MISFIT LIL FIGHTS BACK

Misfit Lil wouldn't allow the rustlers to run off some of her pa's improved Flying G beeves. She started a stampede that trampled them bloodily into the dust. But then two assassins gunned down horse rancher Sundown Sander's son Jimmie. And he had made no move to defend himself, despite Lil's stormy ride to bring him warning. Could devious madam Kitty Malone or gambling-hall owner Flash Sam Whittaker tell the truth about Jimmie's fatal resignation? Lil had to find out.

CHAP O'KEEFE

MISFIT LIL FIGHTS BACK

Complete and Unabridged

LINFORD
Leicester

First published in Great Britain in 2007 by
Robert Hale Limited
London

First Linford Edition
published 2008
by arrangement with
Robert Hale Limited
London

British Library CIP Data

O'Keefe, Chap
Misfit Lil fights back.—Large print ed.—
Linford western library
1. Western stories
2. Large type books
I. Title
823.9'14 [F]

ISBN 978–1–84782–357–1

Published by
F. A. Thorpe (Publishing)
Anstey, Leicestershire

Set by Words & Graphics Ltd.
Anstey, Leicestershire
Printed and bound in Great Britain by
T. J. International Ltd., Padstow, Cornwall

This book is printed on acid-free paper

1

GIRL'S NIGHT OUT

A full moon sailed in clear sky above the rugged peaks of the Henry Mountains far to the arid southwest. It bathed the Flying G range in liquid silver. Nothing much stirred, though Lilian Goodnight, attuned as always to her surroundings, was aware of the nocturnal life of the wilderness, the scuttling of small feet, the stirrings in sage and bunch grass. Rabbits and rodents and grouse. Maybe rattlesnakes.

She'd posted herself a piece back from the rim of a rocky ridge. From the meadow below, occasional bovine murmuring came from a bedded bunch of her father's steers, between forty or fifty head all told. Then an intrusive note entered the night's peaceful symphony.

The unmistakable pound of approaching hoofbeats.

Crouched down, hugging knees clad in buckskin pants, the young woman peered down. Cattle at rest lurched to their feet apprehensively. Irritation rippled through the herd — sign they, too, were aware of strangers arriving on the wanly lit scene.

Backing away from the rim, Lil got to her feet and crossed to where her trusty grey stood patiently on dropped reins. The cow pony she called Rebel was a superb animal she'd trained herself from a foal. Where Lil was concerned, the bronc did anything but live up to his name. She clamped a light hand significantly over Rebel's muzzle, which was warning enough for him not to give betraying voice on hearing the newcomers' horses.

Gathering up the reins, she edged cautiously forward again. Soon enough, Lil discerned something was moving down there. Riders, a half-dozen, slipped from the dusky shadows of a thicket. They spread out and went to work silently except for occasional curt commands to their mounts.

All the cattle were now on their feet, snorting and moving about restlessly. In quick order, the crew began to drift the Flying G herd north from the pasture.

Lil identified the raiders not by name but by their ruffian looks and the general shabbiness of their clothes and saddle gear. They were rustlers . . . range wolves . . . tough and wild men of the outlaw breed of which this remote section of country was seeing a fuller share these days.

I reckon they figure to comb the pasture clean, she thought. What can one girl and one horse do?

The vulnerability of the watched cattle in the newest and worst of lawless times to have confronted the ranching and mining town of Silver Vein and its environs ought not to have been of direct concern to Lil. But she was long done pondering on the incongruity of her motives. Maybe, in spite of all, her lone vigil was inspired by ingrained loyalty to the Flying G brand. That, or a longstanding craving for danger and excitement.

What it wasn't was filial love and devotion . . .

* * *

Miss Lilian had spent her formative years on the Goodnight cattle spread, becoming a regular tomboy in spades. Pa Ben, a widower, eventually found himself out of his depth in handling an impetuous female youngster who could out-shoot, out-ride, out-rope and out-cuss the most high-spirited of his cowpunchers.

Goaded by gossips who hinted at unseemliness even when none was evident, Ben Goodnight sent his growing girl East to a highly respected boarding school for 'finishing' in the European style. When education had done its work, and his rascal daughter was refined, perhaps he could with clear conscience marry her off to a proper, deserving male with the energy of his own bygone youth.

Alas, in Boston Miss Lilian blotted her copybook thoroughly. Wings clipped by the strict rules of the private academy for gentlewomen, she found much-needed exercise and diversion in the forbidden company of an eighteen-year-old gardener's-boy, the only young male on the premises. He was handsome; he was accommodating. Nor was either of them selfish in their pleasure. Together, they made it a sport to enlighten and enliven the drab lives of Lil's colleagues.

The innocent 'young ladies of good family' resorted to a secluded garden shed for initiation into the mysteries of Venus suppressed in their upbringing. Spurred by curiosity and the dares of their peers, the liberated rich girls cast restraint to the winds. For an excited few, the secret new fun became nightly ritual ... till an inevitable lack of caution brought the undesirable augmentation of the seminary's curriculum to the notice of the old maids who ran the institution.

The worn-out gardener's-boy was dismissed and several girls expelled. Among them, Lilian Goodnight was denounced as a ringleader of the 'orgies'. Her pragmatic assertion that the girls couldn't be virgins all their lives and the clean-living boy had been considerate and gentlemanly cut no ice. On instructions from a scandalized board of governors, the headmistress wrote Ben Goodnight charging him with his trollop daughter's punishment.

But, by and large, East was east and West was west.

The less urbanized society wasn't as rigidly based on the double standard of the times, in which a woman who erred against the rule of no intimacy outside wedlock was held a criminal while the man was seen as only an accomplice. Thus, though Lil found a return to life under her father's roof unpalatable and unworkable, her rejection by Silver Vein was far from a given.

Her wearing of mannish attire resumed. She took up again the outdoors accomplishments at which she excelled. A class of folks might despise her unladylike ways, call her a slut no less, but real westerners didn't snub the 'bad girl'. She was a woman — and by their rules any woman was afforded respect whatever her record or station in life.

Duly, young 'Miss Lilian' became 'Misfit Lilian' in recognition of her offence to the Boston academy. And, since nicknames were hardly ever allowed to be longer than what had preceded them, a cut-down handle of 'Misfit Lil' quickly followed.

Lil didn't resent the moniker, nor try to live down her black reputation. She told her pa and anyone who gave her an opening that the Boston headmistress's disgust was a heap of nonsense — though she chose a blunter word — and that a letter from a schoolfriend who'd escaped expulsion made it plain.

'Damned if the hypocrite isn't

keeping our gardener's-boy in a rented cottage,' she would say indignantly. 'The headmistress visits with him nights regular, so's she can take him properly in hand . . . Poor boy! Her hands are like vice-jaws' — Lil sometimes winced here as she pictured particulars — 'and she's ugly as any sin she preaches against.'

★   ★   ★

Lil felt consternation as a burning sickness arose in the pit of her stomach. The Flying G was surely and efficiently being robbed before her eyes. Whatever her relations with her pa, the way of it — the burden of conscience — meant a girl couldn't stand by, doing nothing, and live with herself.

The cattle, lowing and fractious about their disturbance, were being driven off to who knew where. The critters, many of them prime three-year-olds, were prize stock — one of her father's improved herds, cross-bred with imported breeds that bore the names of English counties like Durham and Hereford.

The idea occurred to her in a flash of inspiration, as her best schemes always did. Improved the beeves might be, but they were still part longhorn . . . and spooky as deer. The possibilities in this could literally outweigh the numbers against her. It took little to throw such animals into a panic and hundreds of tons of beef on the move in the wrong direction would provide a powerful argument to make any bunch of rustlers think again . . .

Her mind made up, it was time to fork leather. Action was her inclination and forte. A tall, long-legged girl, Lil took a couple of brisk, circling steps to the rear of Rebel. With a short, exuberant run, she sprang astride, seating herself in the saddle in one smooth, athletic leap. Rebel took off. A press of her knees and a nudge of her heels further urged the horse into a gallop along the rim's edge.

She wasn't bothered that she might be skylined against the moonlight. The cow thieves were fully occupied with their crooked work and the rumble of the beasts' complaints and the thump of their hoofs masked what clatter Rebel made. Nor was the tricky light a difficulty. This country was her country where she'd been born and raised. She knew it as well as a city girl might know each corner of her backyard; every crag, every hole. Her life was here.

The hazed herd was making bellowing, half-hearted progress but Rebel soon outpaced it, putting Lil ahead in the direction the lumbering cows were being driven. She descended from the rim by a narrow trail that might have tested a mountain goat but not the sure-footed grey.

Undetected, she set the plucky horse on a course to confront the approaching herd. Some might have said she was a fool even to consider such a reckless thing, but her plan was decided on, and she was determined to see it through.

As she tore over the pasture and the gap closed, she drew a black-handled revolver. Her thumb automatically cocked it.

Riding down on the herd was going to take all her horsemanship and pluck.

One of the rustlers must have glimpsed her fleeting presence across and through the shifting wall of shifting hide and horns. He raised a cry of astonishment.

'Ain't no nighthawks here. Some nosey cow-waddy, I reckon. Kill or capture 'im!'

'Aw, shuddup, Milt! He's like to git run down and stomped to death!'

But Lil had the dangerous possibilities calculated. She neck-reined her horse, pulling up sharply. She raised the revolver high and let the hammer fall. The gun roared and an orange-red muzzle flash lit up her face.

Had any rustler been close enough to see, they would have recognized her for a dark-haired girl with a good profile, a short, straight nose, full lips, and grey eyes. Not a beautiful face, but pretty enough — bright of eye and healthy-looking.

But only cows saw, and they cared nothing for the sudden apparition. The gun crashed again. Already edgy, the highly-strung critters wheeled sharply from the sight and the sound, as Lil had gambled.

The first person to fall under the turned tide of beef wasn't Lil, but a rustler on the herd's left flank, caught off-guard by its abrupt turn. He and his horse went down like trodden grass, both screaming, to be quickly trampled into flattened, bloodied rags.

Rebel raced to and fro across the path of faltering cattle, heading them off. Misfit Lil fired her gun some more. A wave of panic gripped the milling beasts. They broke into a stumbling run in the direction they'd come, bellowing and roaring with fright.

'That fixes 'em!' Lil exulted.

A considerable scare was thrown into the rustlers; their plans were upset.

Those of the bunch who could, pulled aside from the crazed mass of pounding hoofs and rattling horns. It was like a beef avalanche, engulfing victims and crushing them to blood and gore.

But three didn't disappear under the stolen herd's wild plunge and, as the bedlam of the stampede passed them, they caught sight of Lil.

'Thar he goes!'

'It ain't a he — it's a she!'

'By God, you're right!'

'No matter, we'll get the bitch! Bein' a woman's more the reason we'll throw a loop on her. She'll damn well live long enough to regret this business!'

'We'll bring her down in the dust. Drag the gal, spit on her.'

The leader of the trio, swart and with a bull neck, wasn't so numbed by the shock of the fiasco that had befallen them to see other possibilities. A glint came to his cold eyes. He was the opportunist found in any such lawless group . . . without compunction.

No one was about. The bold,

man-clothed woman, though slim, didn't cut a bad-looking figure. She looked strong enough to withstand vigorous handling. His dust-dry mouth moistened and he licked his lips, anger supplanted by lust.

'Brother, the hell with draggin' and spittin'! Women are born for a whole lot other than that. What's more, we've been the unlucky dogs, goin' short of it too long . . . '

* * *

The surviving rustlers weren't the only parties to have witnessed the stampede. Unnoticed by Lilian Goodnight in the confusion and excitement, another arrival on the scene, tracking the outlaw bunch, had been Jackson Farraday.

On horseback, from cover of a thicket, he observed Misfit Lil's disruptive antics with grim disapproval. His first fear was the pesky girl would get herself killed. His second, when the rustlers were routed, was irritation that his own painstaking investigations into the current bout of local lawlessness would be jeopardized. If the riff-raff were pounded to death under the hoofs of the Flying G herd, his best chance of a lead to their principals — those who orchestrated the growing campaign of anarchy and thievery — would be lost.

He shook his head of long, sun-bleached hair.

'Ground meat will take us nowhere, tell me nothing,' he growled to himself. The Silver Vein country, he appreciated more than most, was on the edge of a declaration of martial law. Matters had got that bad during his short absence.

Jackson Farraday was a weather-burnished scout and guide — a civilian who worked on occasion with the Army. He'd hunted buffalo and supplied meat for railroad construction workers. He'd carried dispatches through hostile Indian country.

His heritage was that of the brave adventurers, pathfinders and mountain men who'd blazed the way to a new America earlier in the century. But he was also an educated man and reputedly spoke seven languages and several Indian dialects. He subscribed to the beliefs of the visionary explorer and lobbyist John Wesley Powell, who promoted scientific survey and the rational use of the West's resources. Rebellion and crime impeded these policies.

Recently, Jackson had been in the Henrys as guide to a noted geologist conducting a study of the unique volcanic features of the Unknown Mountains — for such Powell himself had called the remote range on his visit of 1869, before returning two years later to name it after Joseph Henry, a friend and the secretary of the Smithsonian Institution.

Now Jackson was back, he was shocked to find a return of bad times to the somewhat better-habitated, not so harsh locale that had seemed set to prosper.

'Hell's fire!' he muttered intensely, suddenly. The beginnings of a fresh fear gripped him.

For one of the outlaws had lifted the coiled horsehair lariat from his saddle. He whirled it above his head, building a loop, and raced off to ride down Misfit Lil. With a flick, he hurled the rope at the lone horsewoman.

Lil yelled as the lasso dropped accurately over her head. It settled around her and pinned her arms to her sides. The attacking rustler quickly gave the rope a couple of turns round the steel horn of his saddle to ensure his bet he had her securely. Then he pulled up his bronc sharply. And Lil was wrenched from her seat in the saddle.

Farraday shuddered involuntarily, but was pleased to see the girl wisely kicked her feet free of the stirrups, less an ankle or leg should be dislocated or snapped. She also let herself be jerked clear of her grey's flashing, steel-shod hoofs.

Dust rose high as she struck the hard-baked ground. Farraday could guess the dumping was punishingly, stunningly bruising. He hoped it hadn't broken her neck.

2

A SWIFT RETRIBUTION

The range wolves converged on their fallen prey, whooping gleefully. Lil, still very much alive and furious, lurched on to her knees. She cussed more luridly than a drunken miner.

Jackson heard her assailants' mocking exchange.

'Hush your dirty mouth, gal, or your mom'll have to wash it out with lye soap!'

'Naw ... we can make the sweet thing suck it full o' better suds 'n that!'

Lil finished her tirade passionately. 'You'll be sorry for this, you yellow-gutted bastards!'

One rustler flung down from his horse and hurled himself at her. 'If'n yuh live, missy!'

Rolling her over, he flattened her on

her back and lay on top of her, using his full weight and length to keep her pinned. Excited by her struggles, he wrenched at her fringed buckskin clothing.

Dismounting, his sidewinder side-kicks egged him on.

'That's it, Milt — reckon yuh got holt o' her hawgtight!'

'Hurry it up . . . I'm purty near bustin'-out ready to git my turn!'

'Shove your mitts inside those men's duds! So's yuh can tell it really is all-woman.'

'Naw, strip 'em right off! A bare belly-button ain't near enough. Let's see it all — a jaybird-nekkid filly gittin' poked but good in the dust!'

Milt ripped more buttons off, buckles open and drawstrings loose in a tearing, all-fired rush to be the first to rape the girl who struggled beneath him. The pair became a writhing mass of disarranged pants and kicking legs.

Seeing all this unfold in a matter of scant, heated seconds, Jackson Farraday whipped his long gun from its scarred leather scabbard and fired a warning shot over the attackers' heads. As he did so, he jammed in spurs and raced from the shadows of the thicket concealing him.

The crack of the rifle alone was enough to tell the despicable pack the crime they pursued was discovered. Proven taking of a woman by force was a lynching offence. Milt rose pronto, pulling up his half-mast trousers. They took off for their horses; fumbled for belt-guns.

As Jackson stormed through the whitish moonlight and the still-settling dust from the stampede and the round-up and roping of Misfit Lil, the red eye of muzzle flash winked at him; a gun crashed.

He returned the fire, again aiming to miss.

It was then that Lil took a hand. She staggered to her feet. She kicked free of the loosened, falling noose of rope; rebuckled a belt that hoisted back to lean hips a pair of Colt revolvers cased in tooled leather. And, in a swift, eye-cheating movement, her hands closed on the guns' blackened grips.

Jackson saw the tight set of her face, damp and shiny with sweat except where it was blotched with dust. He knew what she was going to do and he cried out.

'Don't . . . '

But his warning was too late. She brought the guns up, levelling and firing in a continuous blur of movement. The reverberating smash of three close-spaced shots was followed by a short quick silence in which Jackson caught his breath.

Every one of the three rustlers was on the ground — dying, dead, uncontrolled limbs twitching in last spasms. Shirts and vests were splashed with crimson. Blood gurgled in throats and trickled from lips twisted in snarls or by agony. Eyes stared, glazed.

Awed as he always was by the speed and accuracy of Misfit Lil's shooting,

Jackson snapped, 'Why did you have to kill them, Miss Lilian?'

She looked at him incredulously. 'Well, thanks for helping a girl in plenty trouble, ol' pardner, but are you plumb crazy? One of 'em shot at you — you missed him and he was going to shoot again. You saved my hide; I saved yours.'

Jackson felt exasperation. 'But I missed him on purpose. Now I can't follow them and hear them talk. I had a hope they'd spill the beans about the terror on this range.'

'Huh! No nevermind.' Lil nodded curtly at Milt. 'Let's not be squeamish. He'd popped my buttons and put his filthy hand down my pants, on my skin and hair. Hooked fingers up between my legs in point of fact. In my code, men who touch a girl there without leave or say-so are tagged to get their deservings.'

A trickle of cold sweat ran down Jackson's back. What she'd done was ruthless and summary. But in a way,

23

and in a territory where the dominant church still countenanced the likes of plural marriage — once called a twin relic with slavery or barbarism — it was right.

Formal justice for women, other than by the grace of the men who possessed power, was conspicuous by its near absence. God knew how gruelling an ordeal the scum would have gone on to subject Lil to if he hadn't intervened. When they'd tired of their prisoner, they would have disposed of her in a manner or place where her story couldn't be told, or wouldn't be believed.

Would there have been a posse to hunt down her rapists? Unlikely with the weak, undedicated Sheriff Hamish Howard in office. That Lil was no prim, respectable town matron wouldn't have helped either.

Jackson could see reaction was setting in. The girl bit her lip, trying not to let him see her trembling. She'd been very lucky, for it would have been impossible for her to have bested alone three intent, highly aroused attackers. Probably her elation was also tempered now by the horrifying, nauseating evidence of the carnage left in the herd's wake.

She went over to her patiently standing grey horse, unstrapped a canteen, filled her undoubtedly dry mouth and swilled the water around inside bulging cheeks before swallowing.

'Vermin, skunks . . . ' she said under her breath, as though it would further confirm the correctness of the killings in her mind. More audibly, she said, 'I ain't bad hurt.'

Jackson asked, 'Why did you have to go up against them anyhow?' He knew how it was between Lil and the owner of the targeted cattle — her pa. They didn't cotton to each other's thinking on what was best for a girl.

'Someone's gotta look out for the Flying G's interests,' Lil said simply.

'How about your pa's crew?'

Lil's head moved from side to side.

'Real cowpokes ain't like the heroes in Beadle novels. Those stories are bull. With new repeating rifles getting to Angry-fist's renegades again, smaller ranchers have fled their spreads in terror. Cattle wander untended and outlaws take advantage. A cowboy don't put his life on the line for his boss and the brand any more. Not even for forty-five-a-month pay, fresh beef and sono-fabitch stew.'

'True,' Jackson said, and reflected silently that it wasn't so long since Lil and he had put paid to a gun-smuggling operation that had powerfully armed Angry-he-shakes-fist, hotheaded leader of a rebellious Apache sub-tribe. Now, it seemed, their good work was being undone.

A new wave of fear had washed over the Silver Vein country as the re-armed renegade Indians went on the rampage. Abandonment of isolated settlements, and the resulting confusion, were giving rustlers cover and opportunity to make a killing.

In this perilous climate, Lil out of some misplaced loyalty restlessly prowled the boundaries of the Flying G and the rugged canyonlands beyond, largely living off the land, for her skill in wilderness craft was almost equal to his own.

Jackson added, 'But your pa ain't likely to approve of your saving his bacon . . . should I say beef?'

Lil laughed with little humour. 'He knows I don't give a hoot for his opinions.'

'Sure. It's common knowledge your relationship's strained on account of rumours about what you got up to in Boston but — '

'Don't bring that stuff up!' Lil interrupted. 'It wasn't as if I got into any real scrape. Pa made me have schooling I hated. Put a girl in *prison* and you can't expect her to act like a saint. 'Sides, they tried to say I did something I never did. The companions they reckoned I corrupted about lined up for the dispensing of real education.

One right nice boy could scarce oblige so many.'

Jackson sighed wearily. 'I was trying to say your father wouldn't want you violated and dead in any circumstances. And eliminating these small-fry, snakes though they were, doesn't lead us to the smart boss-men who surely lie back of it.'

Lil was forever full of surprises and dilemmas for Jackson. About half his age, she aspired to be a top scout, of worth to the military and others, exactly like himself. Nor was she much short of that capability, an achievement to admire.

But she also idolized him; was that keen to impress him it often became a nuisance and embarrassment. In the West — in the South maybe more so — men did take up with females of tender years, but the practice bothered Jackson. Some future morning, he wouldn't want to wake with a wife beside him still in the spring of life when he was heading into winter.

What Lil said now was a shocker of a different stripe.

'But I already know who these men take their orders from. No one will believe it — leastways, not from me — but I've seen 'em holding secret confabs out on the trail to the canyonlands. And he's the last person anyone would suspect.'

Jackson listened engrossed, absently stroking his neat chin beard. He found Lil's report and theories tied in with facts he'd observed for himself. He said she should return with him to Silver Vein where he'd report the raid and hand over the rustlers' bodies to Sheriff Howard.

'I'll ride some of the way,' Lil agreed. Sensing reluctance, Jackson suggested she might go with him to Fort Dennis to relay her story to Colonel Brook Lexborough, but she baulked at that entirely.

The moon sank and a pre-dawn chilliness cut to their bones in the deepened darkness. Jackson loaded the corpses of the three shot rustlers faces down across their saddles, tying hands to feet. The remains of the men whose bodies had been trampled to formless bits under the pounding hoofs of the stampede, they left. They started out, leading the dead men's horses.

Both were proficient at handling strings of horses, and they made good time in a silence that was companionable but awkward. Jackson didn't like the way Lil's eyes repeatedly returned to him and lingered, dreamily, as though he were leading a goddamned cavalcade in a show.

A pale gold, first light began to streak the eastern sky and broaden. When they were close enough to Silver Vein to see the haze of lights that marked its position on the flats in the lingering darkness ahead, Lil announced her intention to leave him to it.

Jackson reminded, 'It was a busy night and you've ridden a far piece. Are you sure you don't want to go into town for a decent meal and some rest?'

Her dust-streaked face became solemn. She looked deep into his eyes. 'Sure. I'm used to fending for myself and Silver Vein is no more a home for me than anyplace else.'

She turned Rebel quickly then. 'Wish you luck with Sheriff Howard, Jackson.'

Privately, Jackson was half-glad to let her go. Riding into town at dawn with three dead men, heads bobbing to the rhythm of their led horses' uncertain gait, was going to cause enough of a stir. He could cope without the added conjecture liable to be set in train by the company of the notorious Misfit Lil. The story she'd wiped out a bunch of rustlers and he'd packed in some of the bodies was going to get around fast enough. Gossiping biddies would see to that.

On a rising slope, and with the sky taking on fuller colour behind her, she turned back to give a last cheery wave.

No sense in setting your cap, Miss Lilian, he thought. I'm too old. Make up your mind to it. But somehow his resolve to maintain a cool reserve didn't stop him smiling and waving back.

Once she was out of sight, he felt free of a worry.

One worry. For now . . .

★　★　★

Jackson Farraday took himself at the first opportunity to Fort Dennis. At the great wooden gates he announced he had urgent information to convey to the post's commanding officer, Colonel Brook Lexborough.

The civilian scout was well-known to the sentry, a blocky, red-faced veteran with an Irish accent. 'Ver' good, Mr Farrad'y, sor!' he said briskly, and summoned an orderly to escort him across the parade-ground to the stone-built administration block. This was but a formality and courtesy, since Jackson was a familiar figure around the fort.

In Lexborough's spartan office, Lieutenant Michael Covington was closeted with the colonel. The colonel's voice rumbled in earnest conversation. The announcement of Jackson's visit caused it to break off, but both men wore worried frowns which barely lifted.

Covington picked up his spotless tan hat with its crossed-sabres insignia, and Lexborough raised a gnarled but steady hand.

'You may stay, Lieutenant. Farraday might be just the man to advise on what we're discussing.'

Running the stiff, broad hat brim through his hands, Covington said, 'Very good, sir.' His tone held little enthusiasm. From past episodes, Jackson knew it went against the spruce, boyish-looking lieutenant's grain as a graduate of the elite West Point academy to take other than token guidance from a civilian scout.

Lexborough said to Jackson, 'What can I do for you, Mr Farraday?'

'I've intelligence that could tie to the rearming of Angry-fist's renegades, Colonel.'

'Ah! Then I was right, for I was just

assessing the gravity of the troubles with Covington.' Lexborough shook his head. 'We're at our wits' end. Good settlers are leaving. The territory's stirred up as it's never been before. Civilian authority is crumbling and few men dare challenge the anarchy that lets lawlessness thrive.'

The colonel was in his late fifties, heavily built and tall when his long legs weren't jammed under his scarred desk. He had crinkled, iron-grey hair and brains behind his piercing eyes.

Jackson recounted the clash with the rustlers to the two military men. Lexborough listened carefully, nodding occasionally.

'It seems to me wholesale stealing of beef flourishes because of the Indian troubles,' Jackson finished up. 'They clear the way for it and they're encouraged by activities of a white man — a person you'd have thought the least likely to be encouraging them.'

'Eh?' Lexborough said. 'Who's that?'

'His name's Claude J. Frenzeny.'

Covington about spluttered. 'But Frenzeny's the Indian Bureau's agent! I always have favoured the bureau's transfer back from civilian control to the War Department's, but Frenzeny has a duty of care to the reservation Indians.'

Jackson gave a bitter laugh. 'And a lot of care he takes — to feather his own nest!'

Covington went to remonstrate again, but Lexborough put in gently, 'Let Mr Farraday explain, Lieutenant.'

3

KILLERS COME TO TOWN

Jackson pulled up a chair at the colonel's invitation and launched into his report.

'Frenzeny short-changes the Indians, trading the prime, government-issue beef that's their ration for thin, scrub beeves brought him by rogue ranchers and rustlers. He accepts the poor stuff two for one, giving him twice as many critters as he needs. The surplus he channels to a crooked meat-packer in Montana to swell his private pocket-book.'

'But wait!' said Covington, a triumphant gleam in his eye. 'A racket like that wouldn't work. Beef is issued to the Apaches by weight, not by count.'

'Never heard of rigged scales, Lieutenant?' Jackson asked dryly. 'The agency weighs out every beef at six hundred pounds or over, even if it really weighs three hundred.'

'Hmmm . . . ' Colonel Lexborough said, leaning back in his chair and lacing his fingers behind his head. His unseen thumbs circled each other. 'Do we have evidence of this hocus-pocus?'

Encouraged, Covington said, 'Yes, you can't just drag Frenzeny's name into the dirt. Exactly where did you learn this?'

'I've made my own observations from a discreet distance, but Miss Lilian Goodnight has at close quarters eavesdropped on clandestine meetings between Frenzeny and the outlaws who do much of the rustling and driving of stock across borders.'

Distaste showed instantly on Covington's clean-cut face.

'Misfit Lil!' he said with a cutting bite to his tone. 'Then this is unreliable. Telling the unvarnished truth is something Miss Goodnight rarely does if it can be avoided.'

From old, Jackson knew Michael Covington and Lil could seldom be in one place together for long without crossing metaphorical sabres. Why the sparks always flew he couldn't figure, but they did. They were of similar age; Covington was handsome; Lil was pretty — though he guessed tougher than one of the lieutenant's glossy black boots.

'That's not exactly fair, Mr Covington. Lil has her skills and has been of great help to the military here on occasion.'

'Also a damned nuisance,' Covington mumbled, slapping a gauntlet against the yellow seam of his blue trousers till another saving thought came to him. 'Why has the brat said nothing of this before?'

Jackson lifted his broad shoulders. 'Maybe she's kept shut 'cause she knows folks won't believe her. Then again Lil simply ain't one for swaggering around and bragging about what she knows. She's one for bold action.'

Covington put a sneer into his voice.

'I don't doubt her courage, but I do question her wisdom and judgement.'

'Lilian Goodnight is the product of the circumstances into which she was born,' Jackson said, bottling his anger. 'She has wisdom of a different kind. That's what's disagreeable to you. Since her country is where you've been posted, it's too bad you must always repudiate her. Hardship tends to be rude and unrefined, and sooner or later hardship is the frontierswoman's lot.'

Covington's upbringing and education were rooted in the East, where no true lady was capable of the remotest approach to indelicacy of thought, speech or action. The Boston seminary to which Lil had been despatched by her harassed father was paid to instil such gentility; to add the polish of refinement prized by the culture east of the Mississippi River.

But Jackson was aware the West was different — unestablished, under-populated and unrefined. The ratio of men to women was about eight to one in most territories, disregarding some religious and native communities. Women were appreciated solely for the fact of their womanhood.

A woman who'd had more than one lover, who drank whiskey and smoked brown-paper cigarettes that made strong men sick, or who rode astride a spirited bronc, didn't have to be ostracized as a bad lot.

These things Jackson knew but Covington, seemingly, didn't. Of like age, he and Lil should have made a fine pair — they had complementary assets. A promising Army career would be enhanced by a wife who was in her element in the frontier situation. But they were outwardly heartless to each other. It was regrettable, frustrating. Didn't Covington know what he was rejecting? Or was it because he did, and was afraid of it, that he chose to keep the girl at arm's length? An interesting thought . . . and one that disturbed Jackson in a way he wouldn't admit to himself.

Colonel Lexborough harrumphed.

'Old disagreements are beside the point, gentlemen. We've no direct authority over the Indian agency's affairs. Nor should we rely on a young woman — competent or otherwise as she might be and regardless of reputation — as a source of further intelligence. Let's not get our hackles up over comparative irrelevances. Skunk is smelled, it appears, and I'd appreciate it if hard-and-fast facts could be quietly collected . . . '

A short, impromptu conference was held on the doings and status of the Bureau of Indian Affairs' agency in the Silver Vein district.

'Who appointed Frenzeny?' Jackson asked. He pictured in his mind's eye the bloated, paunchy agent — a man who habitually wore an outsize store suit, a derby hat and an authoritative yet falsely hearty manner. A blowhard of sorts.

Lexborough was blunt in telling what he knew.

'Claude Julius Frenzeny was nominated for the post by a gullible

Christian mission with political sway. He has an annual salary of $1,500. His brief is to teach the Indians white practices and oversee assimilation into the civilized, modern world. He carries it out through a system of elementary schooling for children and education in farming techniques for adults to replace traditional subsistence. Washington provides the funds for equipment and the food to keep the Indians from starvation meantime.'

Covington added, 'And if it was all working, that hotheaded hostile Angry-fist would never have broken out of the reservation to make a mockery of the peace policy and create mayhem!'

Jackson nodded to this. 'On which Frenzeny evidently flourishes. He sure spends up in a style which should be beyond the reach of his stated salary.'

He could have added that few had so far shown an inclination to query this. Because Frenzeny was opinionated and had the right connections in high places, he was tolerated by most in

Silver Vein, or simply ignored as an unwelcome reminder of the vexing Indian question.

Lexborough said, 'A good case for further investigation. What do you figure, Mr Farraday?'

* * *

A summer storm with flashes of lightning in the foothills brought Misfit Lil into Silver Vein on the cooling evening breeze that preceded it. She went to McHendry's saloon like any man might, bought a whole bottle of her favourite whiskey — which was imported, top-shelf stuff, not cheap rotgut stocked for undiscriminating waddies — and stationed herself in a quiet corner which gave her a view through the smoke haze and the batwings of the darkening street outside.

Along about nine o'clock by the eighteen-inch dial of the saloon's massive oak-cased timepiece — a product of the Ansonia Clock Company of New York — the arrival of two strangers on the main street caught Lil's interest.

They were tall men on geldings — one a mahogany-bay, the other a dun. Both were hard-faced and had an evil presence. She thought if she could see them closer up, they would have cold, black eyes like lizards. But they carelessly hitched their weary mounts to a rail and went into Kitty Malone's Boarding House, an establishment which didn't so much provide board as a euphemistic front for what was a whorehouse.

With the present disorder in its environs, Silver Vein was a tense and jumpy township. Lil thought such newcomers were apt to put the fear of death into some of its inhabitants, but possibly not Kitty or her more experienced girls. Kitty brought a bastardized version of city sophistication to the West. She sought to recreate the East in a parlour-house, using female charm, a

44

commodity in short supply, to fleece her foolishly co-operative patrons.

When the going got rough, Kitty also had the protection of 'Flash Sam' Whittaker, proprietor of a neighbouring gambling house, the El Dorado, and — Lil just happened to know — of a mortgage on Kitty's house. Thus Whittaker bankrolled prostitution, but avoided the damage that might be done to his name if it were widely known he lived on the earnings of 'unfortunates' and was therefore a pimp.

Lil saw the two strangers each wore Colt .45s low on their thighs, tied down. As well as the breed who bought women by the hour, they looked the type who gunned down men who had prices put on their heads by others. Professional gunmen. Killers . . . They said very little to one another; their expressions if not their body language were inscrutable.

After they'd disappeared into the house, which had heavy, closed red curtains at all its windows, Lil put them

45

out of mind and built a smoke while she fell to pondering the likely tie-up between Frenzeny, the guns that reached Angry-fist's rebellious band, and the rustling operations the subsequent upheaval facilitated. She put a match to the quirly.

She'd passed on her knowledge about the Indian agent to the newly returned Jackson Farraday and she hoped he'd make good use of it. With the reservation Apaches being played for suckers in the matter of beef supplies, she could see how the youngest and proudest bucks might go on the rampage to lift white men's hair.

Her reflections ended suddenly with the reappearance of the two hard men who'd gone into Kitty Malone's. Her grave eyes went to the Ansonia clock. She frowned. The hands didn't quite bisect the big dial. Less than a quarter-hour had elapsed. No time, surely, for a transaction satisfying to men who'd ridden a long ways to get here.

The men stalked across the street,

heading directly and with purpose toward the saloon. Lil recapped her bottle and stowed it in a pocket. She was no coward, but to a smart mind it looked like trouble was in the offing. If she had to head for the hills in a hurry, she might appreciate something to fortify her against coming wet weather.

When the gunslingers pushed through the batwings, Lil saw their pockmarked, sallow faces did indeed have lizard eyes. She figured they were bad, clear through. Two of a kind, their beady gaze swept round the half-filled room.

'Which of yuh is Jimmie Sanders?'

A hush fell. No one said a word, but one patron shuffled toward the door.

The stranger he had to pass closest intercepted him and hit him across the mouth with the back of a hard hand.

'*You* . . . You Sanders?'

'N-no! I ain't him.' Then, more boldly: 'No call to fly offa the handle, mister!'

The second intruder said, 'I don't like lip, feller. Nobody talks to us that way.'

To Lil, it seemed like nobody was talking to them at all, except the one. Folks here were just too scared of outlaw riff-raff these days, let alone clear cold killers.

The man with the quick hand said to his victim, 'I don't like nothin' about you. An' if I don't like a thing, I get rid of it.'

The second man, more shrewd, said, 'Seein's we now know yuh have a tongue, which is more'n can be said 'bout your comp'ny, yuh can talk again, more polite. Tell us who's Jimmie Sanders — son of Sundown Sanders, horse rancher!'

The would-be run-out went to open his mouth, and Lil figured she knew what he was going to say. She wouldn't have chosen to tangle with the menacing pair, but she uncoiled from behind her table and said, 'Jimmie Sanders ain't here!'

The terrorizers looked at her with disdain.

'Hell! A kid in a saloon, Brad! Who

asked you to stick your oar in, whelp?'

The man called Brad said, 'It's a *gal* smokin' an' wearin' men's duds, Phil . . . '

'Well, damned if it ain't so! A tribade mebbe, cross-dressin' an' showin' out with her quirlies an' — ' his eyes fixed on her pocketed bottle of hard liquor — 'drinkin' real men's prairie dew.'

'See here, scantlin',' Brad said, 'we want Jimmie Sanders. If he ain't here or in the cat house, where is he?'

'I don't know,' Lil said. 'If he's wanted legal-like, why don't you go ask at Sheriff Howard's office?'

'It ain't the *law* wants Sanders — it's LOOO. 'Sides, we don't give shit for your chicken-hearted star-packer.'

Lou? Who was Lou, Lil wondered, but these strangers were evidently sufficiently informed to know Silver Vein's sheriff wasn't exactly strong and fearless.

Phil said, 'Forget the freak, Brad. Sport with her can wait till the job's done. Mebbe the gent had more to say . . . '

They turned to the trembling hand who'd tried to light a shuck. Brad said, 'He's my meat.' And he smacked the fellow on the nose with a bunched fist. 'Tell us where we find Sanders!'

The luckless man moaned and blood trickled. 'All right,' he said. 'Don't hit me again! I'll tell you . . . he's prob'ly out at his pa's place — the Diamond S.'

Then he pointed and said the words Lil had hoped not to hear and tried to prevent with her intervention.

'His father's the old gent at the end of the bar . . . Sundown Sanders!'

4

A GROWN MAN CRIES

Samuel 'Sundown' Sanders was ill-fitted to put up a resistance to cold-eyed gundogs and Lil hoped he wouldn't try. Though not a frail man, he was pushing seventy. His face was weather- and life-lined and he still stood straight and tall, but in any fight, the grey-whiskered oldster would be no match for the ugly pair.

A local and liked personality, Sundown had turned from cattle to raising horse in mid-life when Lil had been a button. He'd long since repaid the capital raised to establish his first herds and the tidy Diamond S stables, corrals and breaking pens.

'She ain't much, but she's all mine,' he'd say proudly and with understatement. The improved stock he bred

51

found a good market with traders, cattlemen and the Army. He was also a friend to Lilian Goodnight.

'Door's allus open, gal. Feel free to flop in the hayloft when yuh need it.'

Lil had known his son, Jimmie, for a handsome, happy-go-lucky fellow — very good with skittish horses, of course. The frog walkers, the fence rowers, the pile drivers, the sun fishers, the end swappers . . . no bucker of any kind had him beaten. But his fondness for bronc-busting and wrangling was surpassed by his hankering for high-stakes poker and other games, and women. One woman in particular: Kitty Malone.

Was woman-trouble behind this matter? Lil didn't think so. Leastways, not any ordinary woman-trouble.

Jimmie's weaknesses were the bane of Sundown's contentment. 'Now it looks he's somehow brung real big trouble down on the Diamond S,' Lil thought.

As the two gundogs moved in on Jimmie's pa, she hoped the salty old man wouldn't get a shuck in his snoot, or even be clabber-mouthed about where his son was to be found. Else, the thugs would purely sink their teeth into him and Sundown's spur would be ringing its knell.

The badmen thought they'd scared her with their jeers and threat, but she didn't have any yellow streak. When she bit her sharp tongue, it was because she was waiting a chance. No one was doing or saying anything that would give the strangers an inkling of her bold and brassy rep.

Poor old Sundown tried to stay his accosters' hand.

'Lou, yuh say? Jimmie's never mentioned no Lou. Beg pardon, fellers, but who the hell might Lou be?'

Phil said with heavy emphasis, 'LOOO, Pops. League Of Organized Outlaws.'

Sundown was shaken, but he said bravely, 'Never heard of 'em, sir.'

'You're gonna,' Brad said with a sneer. 'An' I s'pose yuh're tellin' us yuh've seen nothin' of the $5,000 smart li'le Jimmie's helped hisself to from the biggest, most powerful brotherhood in the nation. Well, Pops, we're here to take care of it, yuh unnerstan?'

Lil was fascinated. Always quick on the uptake, she figured Jimmie had crossed a gang of criminals, probably the very ones responsible for backing all that was currently dirty in the Silver Vein country. And the bosses had sent these two killers to exact retribution — remove Jimmie from their rackets just like a normal person might swat a fly!

It was high time she was out of here. She would do for Jimmie what she knew either Sanders guy, father or son, would do for her if she had her back to the wall. She'd have to go warn Jimmie two gunslicks were coming to blow out his lamp. She'd have to do it mighty quick.

Lil edged not for the batwings but past the huge ticking clock to the back of the saloon. She came to a closed door. She reached out a hand, turned the handle and began to ease open the door.

'Where d'yuh think you're goin', sweetheart?' Brad said, a glitter in his eyes. 'We got bis'ness later, remember?'

'You want me with peed pants, mister?' Lil said meekly as she was able. 'I'm busting to get across the yard to the privy.'

Phil cast Brad a black look. 'We got the squawker we need; the dumb bitch ain't nothin' necessary, Brad. Let her go.'

'All right — jest acrost the yard!' Brad rapped.

Lil opened the door wide enough to slip through and was out into the darkness. Exultantly, she vaulted the fence and ran to the livery stable where she'd off-saddled and stalled Rebel.

Sam, the black boy who acted as night hostler, was dozing in the warm atmosphere of hay and manure. He was surprised to see her.

'Lord's-sakes, Miz Lil'n! I di'n't

'spect you back so soon. I jest done give him oats — '

'No nevermind!' Lil cried. She stormed down the straw-littered aisle and dragged her saddle off the rack. She heaved it across her uncomplaining grey mount, who lifted his head to nicker a greeting.

A quick swig from her whiskey bottle, a tightening of the cinch under the horse's belly, and she was up into the hull and on her way.

Sam shook his head. 'That Miz Lil'n ain't nothin' but trouble . . . Sho' is gwine to be trouble somewheres!'

The sky was dark with cloud, approaching night and the storm close at hand in the mountains. Light was poor, but Lil and Rebel knew the trail to the Diamond S well enough to make the tradeoffs between caution and haste at the tricky places.

Swift as Lil had been, she knew LOOO's gundog enforcers and their coerced guide wouldn't be far behind. For Sundown to try thwarting them would take a foolhardy courage. She guessed he'd have to take the bit in his mouth, cruel as it might be, lead the assailants to the Diamond S and his son — and trust to something turning up.

Maybe he'd realized when she'd sneaked out that she herself had a plan in mind to outwit the grim strangers. What an idiot his son had been getting involved with such ruthless scum!

As the miles sped under Rebel's hoofs, the memory of the evil, tough look in the men's killer-eyes kept growing and gaining added significance. They'd be as good — or bad — as any words they'd uttered. Although there was no actual chase, she felt pursued.

Full dark was coming on rapidly and the smell of approaching rain was on the breeze when Lil left Rebel hidden in a thick clump of brush down a branch trail and scooted toward the neat layout of the Diamond S horse ranch.

She walked cautiously toward the main house, keeping to the deepest shadows flanking the stables, the tackhouse and other outbuildings. No telling when Sundown and the outlaw riders would appear. The ranch-house windows were dark and the whole place had about it a gloomy air of vacancy, but after a careful examination, Lil detected an almost-invisible wisp of smoke rising from the rock chimney. Jimmie, or someone, was here, though not making a show of it.

In itself, this was odd, since by his nature, which Lil knew in its broad lines, Jimmie was a young man who liked boisterousness, bright lights and game-playing. What had gone wrong with him these days, she wondered again.

She catfooted across the smoothly packed dirt of the yard to the back door of the house. Lightning flickered, not so far off this time and revealing her empty surroundings in a stark white light. It was followed by a low rumble of echoing thunder in the canyons. In the stables and corrals, horses were made restless. They stomped and whinnied.

Every nerve and muscle alert, Lil stood flat against the split-log wall of the house and raised one hand to the door latch. Just before she quietly called out an inquiry, she heard a sound that gave her pause and set her heart thumping with a new kind of alarm.

Within, a man sobbed quietly and it was not pleasing to a girl's ears. The sound chilled her, speaking as it did with more disturbing eloquence than any words of utter despair. It told of a weariness of heart, a total loss of spirit, of too much to endure without physical expression.

The latch clicked under the pressure of Lil's thumb. The noise was like the cocking of a Colt to her, but went unnoticed by the occupant. The subdued sobbing continued. She eased open the door with bated breath.

Like many rural homes, Sundown and Jimmie Sanders's simple house had one main living space that served as common room and kitchen, utilizing the fireplace for both heating and cooking. Stoves were more familiar in larger and town dwellings.

Jimmie was seated alone before the glowing logs on the hearth, bent over, his face in his hands.

Lil didn't want to intrude on the situation. It embarrassed her, which wasn't a thing easily done, but Jimmie couldn't be left to sit here, indulging in a pitiful grief while men came to kill him.

'Howdy, Jimmie Sanders!' she said loudly, stepping in.

Jimmie froze solid, then dropped his hands from his face, lifted his head and turned reddened eyes on her.

'What do you want, Misfit Lil?' he asked gruffly. 'What're you doing here? You can shelter in the barn if you're a-feared of the rain that's gonna come.'

Gravely, she cut straight to her purpose, pushing aside her puzzlement at the frighteningly black melancholia afflicting him.

'No, Jimmie, I ain't come for that. I've come to warn you to saddle up pronto and ride! Two gents were in town after your blood. They reckoned you've stolen big money from their bosses — '

Jimmie laughed mirthlessly. 'Well, that's a lie, Lilian Goodnight! I did all I was ever asked an' stole nothing from them!'

He made no move to leave his chair by the fire, staring into the flames though it wasn't even cold.

'Whatever you did doesn't matter,' Lil said, agitated by the strangeness of his manner. 'These men are on their way, forcing your pa to bring 'em. What you gotta do is quit the Diamond S and go into hiding. They're gunhawks and I swear they've been sent to kill you!'

Jimmie twisted his lips into a sombre grimace. 'Then let 'em kill me, I say. I'm past all caring now. It'll do me a better turn than it'll do them.'

Lil was out of her depth. To her horror, she heard the tramp of hoofs in the front yard, the jingle of metal bridle pieces as horses were reined in to a halt. A creak of leather. Men's voices.

Time was fast running out to save Jimmie Sanders. It was also starting to rain. The heavy drops were pattering on the roof shingles.

'Leave now!' she urged. 'Out by the back door, before it's too late. You can lose them in the mountains, in the dark and the storm. They don't know these parts. Get away and vanish someplace they can't reach you. Across the Canadian border, or the Mexican . . . think of the flashing-eyed *señoritas*, willing to brighten the hours till this thing here has blown over.'

But one-time flirt Jimmie's looks only grew blacker at mention of romance with the *señoritas*.

'I don't want to go anyplace,' he said despondently. 'Can't you get that into your head, Misfit Lil? Move it on out your ownself, crazy gal . . . and don't come back!'

'Hush that gab!' Lil burst out in

disbelief. 'It's you who's gone crazy, Jimmie Sanders!'

She sensed the worst. That she wasn't going to get him to see the light of sanity; to change his plainly unhinged mind. A dull ache was in her head, and she knew it wasn't because she was feeling the whiskey.

Desperately, she asked him, 'Are you stark loco? Can't you hear them? They're out there with your pa — '

Suddenly, the front door crashed open. Lightning flashed brilliantly. Almost immediately, it was followed by another crash — of thunder — and the rain deluged down.

The eerie light framed three men in the doorway, trying to squeeze themselves through together. Guns at his back, Sundown Sanders was shoved in to fall headlong at his son's feet. He was still alive — thank God! — but the marks of a beating were on his face and a split cheek was bleeding.

'Couldn't hold 'em off no longer, son,' he gasped.

The ugly-humoured hardcases came in behind him, carried on a whiplash gust of wind and wet. Their reptilian eyes were gimlet points behind half-closed lids as they took in the scene.

'If'n yuh're Jimmie Sanders, say your prayers fast, kid!' Brad said.

'I'm Jimmie Sanders,' came the reply without a quiver in a flat, dead voice. 'You didn't have to disrespect my dad. He had nothing to do with this.'

'Hey!' Phil snarled. 'Here's that damn' she-runt from the saloon. What game's she playin'?'

'A smarter one than you brave *caballeros*!' she retorted with defiance she had to work hard to muster. 'Beating up an elderly gent — '

Brad snapped, 'The hell with the silly bitch! Our orders are to rub this cheatin' bastard out.'

Thus were Lil and her tongue-lashing dismissed from their calculations. And Lil's last hope against hope that the gundogs might allow Jimmie to live was dashed.

Jimmie made no attempt to grab for a weapon, though guns and a shell-belt hung from pegs on the ranch-house wall. He sat impassively in the chair, not attempting to rise.

The execution — for that was what it was — was carried out with no more preliminaries. A new flash of lightning showed the visitors' faces, set and white as death-masks. They were confident in their command of the horrific situation. They were its authors.

They levelled their six-guns, and each cold-bloodedly fired hot lead into Jimmie's undefended body.

5

LIL FIGHTS BACK

Lil was shocked that it had happened so swiftly — before, in fact, she could make up her own mind about what she had to do.

Unlike the hapless victim, resigned to death with a kind of fatalism, seeming to embrace it, Lil fought back.

As Jimmie was punched out of his chair, to bleed on the floor from what would be rapidly fatal, close-range gun wounds, she drew, cocked and fired a .45 of her own.

Her shot slammed into Brad's chest, spinning him round and exiting raggedly in an explosive gout of red from his right shoulder. He dropped his gun and crumpled to the floor.

The only thing he had time to mumble this side of hell was an incredulous, 'She got me! The bitch can use that iron . . . '

Phil had no more figured Lil's play than his partner.

'Goddamn!' he spat. He was unnerved, either by the unexpectedness, Lil's proficiency, or his fury. His swinging gun cut loose, but the slug whistled past Lil's diving head.

Lil felt only the hot wind of the passing slug. She hit the floor and rolled like a big cat. Armed not with claws but her gun, Lil showed her deadshot skills a second time.

Phil had no chance for last words, let alone attempt a better-aimed second shot of his own. Her bullet drilled a third, dark eye through his forehead and sent a fine spray of blood, bone and brains across the room.

The reverberations of gunfire were drowned in a new roll of thunder. His persecutors wiped out, Sundown Sanders lurched groggily to his feet.

'Hell, gal, that was some shootin' . . . '

'But Jimmie's dead, too, Sundown — I couldn't save your son,' Lil said brokenly. 'What was it with him? He wouldn't even try to save himself. I don't understand.'

Sundown put a calloused, consoling hand on her shoulder, though his own eyes were filled with tears.

'Don't even try, Lil gal. Thar's gonna be more trouble. Get offa the Diamond S your ownself. I can loan yuh a slicker, if'n yuh haven't brung one. I'll bury these varmints an' poor Jimmie, too. No one need know nothin'.'

Lil rejected the proposition. 'But the folks who know nothing will include me,' she said with a trace of irritation. 'What was wrong with Jimmie, Sundown?'

Though almost instant justice had been dealt to Jimmie's killers, the mystery was unsolved. Jimmie knew he was about to meet his death, yet instead of running like his pants were on fire, he'd awaited his executioners like he was resigned to his fate. Like life wasn't worth living.

Sundown sighed deeply. 'Can't say, gal.' Then, as though realizing he owed her something, he essayed the beginnings of an explanation.

'Way back he'd been losin' heavily at faro in Flash Sam's El Dorado gamin'-room. Were to the tune o' nigh on three thousand dollars. Flash Sam held his IOUs in that amount. I paid 'em off in full but tol' Jimmie thar'd be no more. He swore on the Bible he'd gamble no more.'

Lil frowned. 'So did he? Did he somehow get hold of the gang's missing $5,000 to pay off a new gambling debt?'

'Don't think so,' the old timer said, shaking his head. 'Leastways, never saw anysuch money an' I don't think Jimmie went back to Flash Sam's. Can't tell more, Lil . . . guess it'll have to be let lie.'

'It ain't good enough,' Lil said, her eyes stormy as the night sky outside. 'I want to know who and what was behind these paid killers. I aim to find

69

out how Jimmie ran foul of the outlaws — exactly what kind of cards got stacked against him this time.'

Sundown's voice trembled. 'Easy, Lil. The owlhoots've gotten the run o' the Silver Vein country.' He was despairing. 'Jimmie gone! Them rubbin' out you likewise'd be a bitter business . . . a sight more'n I could stand. Drop the idea, y'hear?'

She made a fierce gesture with her smoke-reeking Colt and jammed the weapon back into its holster.

'Damned if I will! I'm gonna work this murdering mess out! I already got some ideas I can follow up.'

'But they're killers, Lil. Rotten-mean an' snake vicious. Yuh'll get about the chance of a celluloid doll in hell!'

But Lil wasn't taking any notice of his protests. She was out the door and running back to where she'd loosely tied Rebel. 'Me a celluloid doll?' she muttered crossly. 'The grizzly porcupine! I never did hear such a low-down-ridiculous notion.'

'Hey!' Sundown yelled after her. 'What about the slicker?'

★   ★   ★

Jackson Farraday had been scouting due south in the vicinity of a remote Indian agency building on a stretch of the stage road out of Silver Vein. The structure at Javelina Bend was a raw, seemingly unoccupied log cabin, grandly called a sub-office and placed there for the receipt of mail, though not much else.

Jackson had been trying to build up his case — which was still no more than an unsubstantiated theory in point of fact — that shady links existed between Claude Frenzeny's activities, the Indian unrest and the rustling. But the storm had put paid to his hopes of observing anything, such as a rendezvous of the kind reported by Lilian Goodnight, which would be apt to constitute evidence.

Overnight, buttoned to the neck in

his slicker, he'd been obliged to seek shelter. He'd descended partway into a gorge where the leeside wall had protected him from the full blast of wind and rain in an otherwise forbidding and precarious campsite.

Come daybreak, and the passing of the bad weather, he headed back toward town with the abating wind on his back and the rumble of the night's thunder reduced to a low growl among far-distant peaks. Wanting to keep his investigations confidential, he swung away from the stage road, following rugged backtrails through warped and folded geological formations where the colours of the eroded rock changed spectacularly from black and yellow to white and red.

He topped out on a ridge overlooking a spread of sage, sand and piñon and the occasional juniper . . . plus the Diamond S horse ranch.

Thereupon his gaze happened to be drawn to the buildings, where back of the main house a man was shovelling the dirt — hereabout a fine mix of sand and clay and a rare colour of red.

'That's ol' Sundown Sanders digging down there,' he told no one but himself and his bronc. 'Don't seem right.'

After a pause to blow his horse, Jackson rode down.

He tipped his hat in a friendly salute. 'Howdy, Sundown. Not meaning to intrude, but ain't that hard work for a man of your years? Where's Jimmie, and what are you doing?'

Sundown dropped the spade, lifted his own hat and mopped sweat from his brow.

'Jimmie's gone, Farraday. Dead, an' I buried him first.' He waved a hand to where a fresh mound of dirt stood under a grove of whispering aspens bordering the front yard. 'Now I'm makin' the holes to plant the roosters that kilt him.'

Shocked, Jackson expressed his condolences over Jimmie and gently prompted the old man to go over again what he'd said, to sketch in more detail and get the straight of it.

'That's mighty bad, Sundown, but you don't have to bury these bastards.'

They'd retreated into the shade of the barn where Sundown had dragged the hardcases' corpses.

'Sure I do. Unmarked graves, so no one knows or c'n find 'em. Else this goddamned LOOO is liable to send more killers — to kill *their* killer. I ain't no man's fool, an' I c'n figger that.'

'Who did kill 'em? Jimmie? You?'

'Nope. Jimmie didn't do nothin', an' I lost m' gunspeed way back. It were Misfit Lil. The gal's red hell on wheels with a shooting-iron!'

'Lilian Goodnight?'

''Sright. She were in McHendry's when the gunhawks showed an' took it inta her fool head to play a hand.'

Jackson nodded gravely. 'That sounds like Lil. I allow she's fast as any gunfighter I ever saw. And got a nose for trouble.'

'Like I'm a-feared,' Sundown growled unhappily. 'She's ridden off threatenin' to stick it in a heap more. So now do yuh savvy why I'm buryin' the evidence?'

'I think I do.'

'That gal opens her mouth an' folks is gonna know. Bad 'nough my son gone, I don't want her death on my conscience to boot. It would weigh considerable. I seen her make them two gunslicks look like hamfisted greenhorns — oh, she's a deep 'un an' plenty fast on the gun-throw! — but I'm mindful she's no more'n a gal. An' I never did cotton to the way she goes about wearin' men's pants . . . '

Appalling and puzzling though Jimmie's death was, Jackson, too, didn't want the distraction — the worry — Misfit Lil's interventions in dangerous set-ups always seemed to cause him.

Then again, he had a hunch information on the identities of the two unknown executioners could shed light on the greater pattern of lawlessness he was probing undercover for the military. Did the missing $5,000 Jimmie had been accused of grabbing connect with the gun-running, the rustling and other rackets?

'Could be worthwhile head money on this outlaw trash,' he said, nudging one of the bodies with a toe.

'Don't want a plugged nickel of it!' Sundown snapped. 'Pos'tive sure it'd do me nor Lil no good a-tall.'

Jackson said calmly, 'I want to know who they were. I got my reasons. I've packed bodies of outlaws into town before — just recent, truth to tell. Sheriff Howard might have paper on this pair. There's more than one way of skinning a cat. What if I tell a white lie? Put it around they tried to ambush me and I shot back and got the better of them?'

Sundown was nervous but finally gave his cautious co-operation.

'Shucks, 'taint no favour, yet it do save me the buryin' of 'em, so suit yuhself, Farraday . . . But I'm trustin' yuh to make no slip-ups, mind.'

★ ★ ★

The night's heavy rain still stood in glutinous pools in the ruts of Silver Vein's main street. When the sun got to it, it would steam. The squelching muck stuck to the hoofs of Jackson Farraday's and the dead excecutioners' horses as he brought the bodies into town.

Jackson had no high hopes of active assistance from Sheriff Hamish Howard. A sorry excuse for a peace officer, the catching of votes came higher on Howard's list of priorities than the catching or identifying of outlaws.

Not for a first time, Jackson had cause to note that the reward and wanted posters tacked to the walls of the sheriff's office in Silver Vein were brown and curling from long exposure to sunlight that for the best part of the day was indirect.

Howard preferred sitting at his desk to sitting a saddle. And the chair was furnished with a plump cushion.

'There must be later notices than these,' Jackson told him, flinging a dismissive hand toward the discoloured rogues' gallery.

Howard was big and running to fat. He had thin lips between flabby jowls. He pursed them in disapproval of the implied criticism and swelled up his chest beneath a tight, conspicuously tin-badged leather vest.

'There are some,' he allowed heavily. 'They been — uh — filed in the bottom drawer of the secr'tary.'

'Better than in the wastepaper basket, I guess,' Jackson said, his tone acid. 'Can I go through them?'

The drawers were under the writing-desk part of a seldom-used piece of mahogany furniture that looked out of place tucked in the darkest and dustiest corner of the sheriff's office.

'Help yuhself, Mister Farraday,' Howard grunted. 'Ain't it comin' a kinda habit, this luggin' of dead 'uns inta town?'

Jackson noted the disparagement, didn't answer but got to his knees. He pulled out the drawer and began

78

shuffling through the undisplayed dodgers.

He understood the set-up here perfectly. No benefit would accrue to Howard from recognizing wanted men's portraits. As an elected official, he wasn't permitted to claim bounties. Were fugitives to show in his bailiwick — as many riding the Outlaw Trail indubitably did — Howard would consider it foolish that he'd obliged himself to risk his neck for no profit. So the papers were hidden from view and he got on with safer 'law enforcement', like gathering taxes and fees, percentages of which were his personal due of office.

'Couldn't put a name to either o' the rats m'self,' Howard said.

'Did you see them alive — when they were in town?'

'Nope. An' what if I had? They'd committed no crime in my county at that point.'

'They went to Kitty Malone's, I was told.'

'Ain't no wrong in that,' Howard said, beginning to bluster. 'I visit with Miss Malone, too. On business — to c'llect tax. She's *legal*, notwithstandin' old ladies' whinin'.'

Jackson didn't need to question Howard on that score, but he liked to needle the lazy fat fool. He knew the town had ordinances which could shut down its bawdy houses, notably Kitty Malone's, if the local bigwigs chose to demand their enforcement. They did not, and to ensure the sheriff's complicity, allowed him to impose a tax. The madams paid Howard weekly $10 per house and $3 per 'boarder', allegedly to cover regular medical examinations and to see the peace was kept by patrons.

Toward the bottom of the drawer, Jackson found the papers he was looking for, folded together. Philip Ketchum and Bradley Roach worked as a team, it appeared. They were accused of killings and robbery while acting as enforcers for a beef-packing company

in Montana which had labour troubles.
Montana again!

The rustlers Misfit Lil had wiped out
with her stampede had ridden horses
with Montana brands . . . and the girl
reckoned Claude Frenzeny had dealings
with an outfit in Montana that asked no
questions.

A pattern was starting to emerge
from all this, Jackson was sure. But
where did Jimmie's death, the intimi-
dating LOOO, the running of guns to
hostile Indians and a missing $5,000 fit
in?

'Found 'em,' Jackson announced to
Howard. He held the dodgers with
their crude but identifiable pictures
aloft. 'The warrants are out sure
enough.'

The sheriff scratched his armpit and
looked over with as much apprehension
as interest.

'Dawggone. Why, that's jest fine 'n'
dandy fer yuh, Mister Farraday. I'll file
application in your behalf fer the
bounty on the sonsofbitches. Yuh'll git

the *dinero* an' then this crap'll be over.'

With the key questions unanswered and the Silver Vein country still in the grip of lawlessness, Jackson didn't think it would finish that easily.

6

CHINA DOLL

True to her word to Sundown Sanders, Misfit Lil was following lines of inquiry of her own.

She was an inveterate observer of life in Silver Vein and around, as well as in the wilderness of the canyonlands. To each, she applied her curiosity in ways best-suited to place and circumstances. She seldom missed anything of interest. The few like Lieutenant Michael Covington who dared to call her a bothersome baggage to her face, were rewarded with appropriate retorts. To the lieutenant (whose handsome looks set average Silver Vein maidens blushing) she would say sweetly but sarcastically, 'Oh, Mike, would you break *my* heart in two?' The diminutive 'Mike' he hated as disrespectfully familiar.

Lil wanted to find out what had sparked the ruination of Jimmie Sanders's cheerful nature, bringing him to dejection and withdrawal into himself. To a chilling readiness to embrace death.

She hit upon Kitty Malone's boarding house as being a good place to start casting about for sign of the trail that had led to the likeable fellow's horrific demise. Her wide knowledge of local affairs told her Jimmie had been wont to spend a couple of nights a week in town at Kitty's.

The whispers of busy mouths had it Jimmie had a fondness for Kitty herself — 'she'd gone to his head,' the gossips said — but her premises were obviously not a place where you could sail in and ask questions of a private nature.

A possible answer to Lil's difficulty presented itself in the distinctive person of Suey-Ling, one of Kitty's youngest girls. Conveniently, Lil had struck up a friendship of sorts with Suey-Ling after meeting her in the Goldbergs' general store. They had two things in common — both were ostracized by much of the community and both wore trousers.

Lil was checking out the boarding house from the thick scrub that bordered its back yard when Suey-Ling's unmistakable figure emerged from a rear door. Kitty's girls strolled in the yard for their exercise and some to smoke. Lil reckoned their hired-out bodies probably got enough physical use and tobacco fumes inside the house, but likely they could do with the air.

Lil called softly from her concealment. 'Psst! Suey-Ling, over here! I need to talk to you . . . '

Slim and youthful, Suey-Ling was simply clad in a long-sleeved, high-necked jacket of dove-grey silk, bordered with black, and quaint trousers of the same material. She wore no bonnet against the sun, like most town ladies did, and her black hair was smoothed down over her head and wound into a knot behind.

She stepped over to the high scrub,

daintily and cautiously on embroidered slippers.

'I will talk with you, Miss Lilian,' she said in a sing-song way. 'This only because the madam, Miss Kitty, out. She does not approve working girl conversing with ordinary girl.'

'I'm not an ordinary girl, Suey-Ling. And I'm your friend.'

'That true. You not like town women but child of wild country. Though Miss Kitty be angry, I will talk. I give to friends and take from enemies.'

Lil thought Suey-Ling had the symmetry and perfection of an exotic flower. Her face was smooth, white rather than olive, with high cheekbones below almond-shaped eyes. But the Oriental girl's delicacy of looks and manner belied what Lil knew was her sad and rigorous life. A timid or fragile creature wouldn't have survived the ordeals she'd gone through.

Her philosophy wasn't always easy to follow.

'I reckon you should quit Miss

Kitty's,' Lil said. 'In her house, you have to give like it or not, surely.'

Suey-Ling folded small and well-formed, butterfly hands in front of her as though in supplication. She cast down her lovely eyes.

'I want only to go home, which not possible. It not so bad as other place. Here, I learn to pretend pleasure — I take it when I desire and I give it when I must. After the thing is done, whichever way, there can be neither giving back nor taking back.'

The reply was as soft and meek as the cooing of a dove, albeit a soiled one.

Lil had learned Suey-Ling's story in earlier talks. She'd been a gift to Kitty Malone from Flash Sam Whittaker. He'd bought her from a previous 'owner', a San Francisco procurer who'd put her to work in the Chinatown cribs of the Barbary Coast after she'd arrived by ship — one of thousands of slave women who over the years were forcibly taken from their homelands across the sea.

In America, Suey-Ling had first spent two months in a cell-like cubicle, whence her owner introduced men who'd paid him to do as they willed with a 'China doll'. A sordid bill of fare had set separate charges for looking, feeling and the rest. When she'd been regarded as appropriately subordinated and educated, her person rather than her use had become an article of western commerce.

At Kitty Malone's house, she was required to entertain men by the hour or the night; was provided more civilized room and board; was allowed to sew new clothes. Discriminating men considered her alien allure a fresh diversion in Silver Vein.

Lil said, 'I want to talk about Jimmie Sanders. You know the man I mean?'

The barest flicker of emotion betrayed Suey-Ling's apprehension. 'They say this Jimmie die. I not *know* him. He always ask for Miss Kitty herself, who want biggest money to lie with any man.'

Lil thought of the $5,000 . . . but

that was ridiculous. No woman's favours could command prices that would add up to that, unless maybe he bought them for all night, every night for nigh on a year, excluding the days of indisposition.

Hitting on another thought, she asked, 'Did Miss Kitty admire to be with Jimmie?'

Not meeting Lil's eyes, Suey-Ling said, 'I think she laugh at him behind back. She encourage him for reason I not understand. I listen. When he say he have no money, she say Jimmie must help her in return. Jimmie, he say this hell of dangerous job, apt to get man strung up by neck, but he do anyway because he love her to death.'

Lil's eyebrows shot up an inch. Now this was interesting!

'Do tell . . . ' she murmured as Suey-Ling came to an abrupt stop.

The pretty Oriental shrugged her slim shoulders. 'I have tell you all, Miss Lilian. Now I must go and you must ask questions in another place.'

Suey-Ling turned abruptly, indicating the palaver was at an end. She glided back to the house, concerned no doubt that she'd be missed and questioned by her colleagues.

Lil felt sick at heart. Despite his gambling and womanizing, Jimmie had been no man of the world. To her thinking, anyone who made bargains with Kitty Malone was asking for trouble. The woman was unscrupulous, remorseless, operating in a game where success relied on bamboozling suckers. Kitty would've found it easy to take Jimmie for a ride quite different from the one she gave him. It sounded like her interest in Jimmie had been in the way of business of some kind, and she'd been cold to his sincerity.

Lil backed away through the crackling thicker brush, then flitted almost silently through the empty lots behind its screen.

If Suey-Ling knew Jimmie was dead, so would Kitty Malone. What would she be thinking of *that*?

Reckless and forthright as she was, Lil decided she'd make it her business to know. The madam didn't scare her like she did most of her girls. She also guessed where Kitty Malone would be found: at the El Dorado, the gaming house that was the headquarters of its owner, Sam Whittaker. 'Flash Sam'.

★   ★   ★

Whittaker had risen in less than a decade from near rags to riches, motivated by naked greed and without scruples. He ran the sweetest rackets in town. Kitty Malone's establishment functioned under his discreet purview.

Lil detested Flash Sam and everything the man stood for. These days he cut a dandified figure in his perfectly tailored clothes. Last time she'd seen him, he'd worn a burgundy frock-coat and calf-length boots of finest Morocco leather polished to a glowing sheen. A pearl-grey Stetson had been set at a jaunty angle over slicked back and heavily pomaded hair, which also ran down in dark sideburns to a square jaw. He sported a black line of moustache above heavy, sensual lips.

In Flash Sam, dapper dress and foppish grooming disguised a well-fed, muscular body wherein lurked a vicious and prideful arrogance.

Kitty Malone was beholden to Flash Sam and therefore visited with him frequently in his office and living quarters, upstairs back of the El Dorado. Lil considered they made a fine matching pair, pulling a showy but tawdry wagon. Both deceived men who sought diversion from workaday toil in the town. Gambling was the great American pastime; prostitution, they said, was the world's oldest profession.

The El Dorado was no common saloon. It had no typical falsefronted façade, but presented itself as a gaming club for gentlemen with entry to its genuine two storeys of chance and glitter allegedly by invitation. This was a farce, since the facts were any man with a full wallet or poke — plus maybe an unadmitted willingness to be fleeced — was welcome to pass within its portal, grandly but incongruously framed by white Grecian columns like a southern plantation's mansion.

House percentages were high and policy — the lottery-type game popular elsewhere with small bettors — wasn't offered, though poker, faro and roulette were. Adroit staff concentrated on encouraging high stakes and free spending.

Misfit Lil passed through the massive, oaken double doors — no batwings here! — and straight into Flash Sam Whittaker's stronghold. But she got no further than the carpeted lobby before her arm was grabbed by the sneering, heavily muscled assistant on door duty.

'What're you doing in here, brat?' he challenged.

Unflinching, Lil said, 'I want to see Miss Kitty Malone and I believe I might find her here.'

'Miss Malone has business with the chief; she won't want to see you here, Misfit Lil,' the man scoffed. 'Nor any place, I reckon. If'n it's a job you're after, no one in this bailiwick is gonna pay to poke a skinny-shanked shrew with a known tart tongue!'

Lil swallowed her pride. She pretended to ignore the cold malice of the thug's tone and the several insults he'd delivered.

'So I've come to the right place. Maybe I'll wait just over there on that sofa.'

The guard eyeballed her. His eyes were small, dirty, deep-set and snake mean. 'Vamoose! Light a shuck!'

'Suppose I've been sent to find Kitty Malone by Suey-Ling, who's one of her girls?'

The guard saw through her lie, and smiled threateningly. 'Suppose nothing! No one wants to see you, kid, ever. You're a busybody and a mischief-maker. Get the hell outa here before I break your arm!'

Lil was angry — deep-down angry — but knew her first line of approach had been thwarted. And Lil being Lil, that didn't mean she was about to give up. She'd have to try a different tack.

Meekly, she let the doorman do his job. He marched her to the entrance and pushed her out on to the plankwalk outside.

'Scram, missy,' he said. 'We don't want the likes of your trash in here. Quit your fool games and your damn snooping!'

Lil brushed her sleeve where he'd held her. Then, after a moment loaded with venomous tension, she strode off, head in the air.

But she went no further than a block. She turned right into a dog-trot between buildings, picked her way over some garbage, and turned right again. This brought her alongside the high fence that enclosed the yard back of the El Dorado.

She took a short run at the fence and, long legs propelling her to a great spring, was up and over it in a high jump. She dropped down lightly on the other side and scooted into the cover of a cluster of trash barrels.

She stayed there several moments, heart thumping, listening for the cries of outrage that might tell her the unorthodox and daring entry had been observed.

Nothing . . . But yes, there was something. She caught the sound of stifled laughter, splashing water and low voices. Two people, seemingly a man and a woman, enjoying themselves.

Lil thought it all very interesting.

But her other thought — that her tenacity of purpose was not anticipated — proved to be mistaken.

7

IN HOT WATER

Lil was intrigued. The sounds of intimate merriment merited the closest inspection. She fixed the point of origin as a large window with leaded, stained glass inserts on the upper floor.

In comparison with how she'd been received at the front of the El Dorado, entry at the rear was ridiculously easy. An unlatched window gave access to an unoccupied storeroom and a back staircase.

She moved silently up the stairs, got her bearings in relation to the outside and went down a passage to the left. The sounds of low voices and splashing grew louder. She peeped through the crack of a door left slightly ajar and was rewarded with a scene she found highly informative.

The business Kitty Malone had with Flash Sam was being conducted in a bathroom of a kind Lil had seen in Boston but was rarer in frontier towns, where baths were mostly taken at ground level, in a shed, a fenced yard or a kitchen.

From the steam, it was obvious an ample supply of hot water had been placed in the room.

Kitty's outdoor cloak was mingled with a pile of male clothing on the floor. With her back to the door, on her knees, the madam was attired in her usual boarding-house style, which was in the stuff a dance-hall belle might wear. Considerable black stocking was visible below the hem of a spangled skirt, now stretched to seam-straining point over a voluptuous bottom.

Flash Sam was sitting and soaking in a high-sided, free-standing copper bathtub.

Kitty was beside the tub. Laughingly, she leaned forward to rub a bar of soap over his hairy chest. Her full-blown figure looked set to explode into his face out of the corseted, low-necklined bodice into which it was packed.

'Careful, Kitty dear — you'll get yourself wet,' Flash Sam said.

'I'm wet already,' she said. 'Where it matters.'

'You're a wicked, savvy woman,' he scolded playfully.

The general belief around Silver Vein was that Kitty Malone was indebted to Flash Sam and under his thumb. If that was the case, plainly from what Lil was seeing and hearing here the situation didn't bother Kitty. And if Jimmie Sanders had pressed his suit to Kitty in the belief she considered him more than a client, he'd been duped. With Jimmie barely gone, Kitty was happily administering to a principal who, it appeared, was also a lover.

It was enough to appal a cynic. Kitty Malone was a voracious, double-dealing wanton, she decided.

Lil's eyes widened as Flash Sam

stood up in the tub. He was burly, thick-set, and, of course, flagrantly naked. Half-amused, she calculated he was inches bigger than a gardener's-boy in Boston.

He bantered, 'A sky-pilot told me the Bible makes it clear that if a woman washes someone's feet and dries them with her hair, she's humbled herself in a suitably Christian way.'

Kitty laughed and slapped at him playfully.

'Feet washing?' she said incredulously. 'We can do better than that, can't we, big boy?'

'God, Kitty, you know we're gonna!'

His brilliant state of readiness and the fascinating bob Kitty had produced fairly took Lil's breath away. She was almost taken unawares.

But an abrupt movement in the tendrils of steamy air drifting from the bathroom made Lil turn instinctively, and the swinging gun barrel aimed at her head swished past. If it had hit, her skull might have been cracked like an egg-shell. The heavily muscled door-man who'd already thrown her out was pussyfooting only in the way he'd sneaked up the stairs to surprise her.

Sidestepping the blow, Lil with a lithe quickness chopped at his biceps with the hard edge of her left hand. It was a big target and it was testimony to her fighting skills that she hit exactly the right spot. She'd learned the skills well from spying on many a bunkhouse scrap at the Flying G in her tomboy years; had tried some of the blows and throws with friendly hands till her father had put a stop to it. ('Why, Dad? I've never gotten hurt.')

The big man staggered with a grunt of pain. His arm was suddenly paralysed from shoulder to wrist. The gun fell from his nerveless fingers, thudding to carpeted floor.

Lil followed up her advantage.

She delivered a creditable right uppercut which impacted on the point of the big man's jaw. His head snapped back on his thick neck and he started back-pedalling automatically down the passage toward the back stairs.

Lil lunged after him, knowing she couldn't stop now. She had to get past him, down the stairs and out of here. She lowered her shoulder and drove it into his broad chest.

The heavy thug stumbled backwards into the balustrade that edged the passage where it reached the steep stairwell. Carpentry in this part of the building was definitely less ornate, maybe flimsier, than in the rooms open to the El Dorado's patrons. The rail broke apart under his stumbling weight in a shower of splinters and flying balusters.

Balance lost, he went over backward, almost in slow motion. He let out an anguished yell and somersaulted helplessly down the house-deep well, hitting the treads once, about halfway down. He bounced; hit the floor at the bottom with a crash that shook the walls. He stayed in a buckled heap, groaning and unable to pick himself up.

'Damn you . . . Busted me, bitch.

You've busted me bad.'

But Lil wasn't away free.

For, in that instant, with little warning other than the knowledge he and Kitty Malone had been in the bathroom behind her — must have heard the sounds of struggle besides the house-rattling fall of the guard — a bare-skinned Flash Sam flung a thick, fluffy towel over her head.

'A dirty snooper, Kitty! But I got her.'

'Misfit Lil!' Kitty cried. 'What the hell's the artless hooker doing here?'

'Slinking in where she ain't welcome, for sure!'

Flash Sam tightened his hold on Lil cruelly, grabbing a breast with thick fingers that dug in deeply and bruisingly. She struggled furiously to no avail. She tried to tear the towel away; she kicked back at him. But the towel was tightened smotheringly. She couldn't breathe.

Long seconds dragged into a minute. More.

'Hell, she's thrown Burt down the stairs!'

The vile grip on her chest was augmented by constricting bands of pain in her air-starved lungs.

'*She's a sticky-beak! What did she hear? How much does she know?*'

Ripe oaths were sworn but the clinging towel muffled what they were saying. Its ends were twisted round her neck. She was choking and burning hot.

Then — horror! The continuing absence of oxygen meant she couldn't fight back at all.

A laugh echoed in her skull. '*She's only a woman, and a woman's strength's soon exhausted!*'

Her limbs went to jelly and she was losing all consciousness. Only blackness was before her eyes; only roaring in her ears . . .

★   ★   ★

Jackson Farraday concluded his business with Sheriff Hamish Howard. It wasn't entirely to his satisfaction, since the lawman saw no reason to make inquiries about why the pair of dead gunnies had been in Silver Vein, or why they'd killed Jimmie Sanders.

Jackson didn't, of course, encourage him to ask about how Philip Ketchum and Bradley Roach had 'ambushed' him and met their deaths. Not that such encouragement would have made a jot of difference to a man of his ingrained slothfulness.

Lilian Goodnight had said on a previous occasion the ol' coot didn't have the guts to go up against ruthless criminals. She called him Sheriff *Coward* and reckoned he had a heap to learn about lawdogging. What Howard did know was how to keep himself out of trouble, buy votes and gather in the fees and taxes. A huge percentage of the latter, as much as fifty, constituted a lucrative personal cut, and made him scarcely better than a robber.

Jackson remembered his promise to Sundown Sanders. He'd said he'd look out for Lil; try to see she didn't poke her nose into affairs that might prove dangerous. Proficient as the 'Princess of Pistoleers' might be with her guns, the old man was right to be concerned about the girl's safety. Hired killers had been sent into the country and had murdered Sundown's son. Their own demise was no assurance their bosses, the shadowy LOOO, wouldn't send in more assassins . . .

But Lil was nowhere to be found.

Since she had no ties and lived almost free as a bird, her comings and goings were apt to be erratic, untellable. Jackson thought little of it for a full day.

The second day brought no sign of Lil and the beginnings of deeper concern. Something Sundown had said suggested to Jackson he should check out Jimmie's old haunts in Silver Vein, to see if Lil had been seen at any of them, poking in her nose as she'd vowed she would to the young man's father.

The process lickety-spit brought him to Kitty Malone's girls' boarding house, where Jimmie had allegedly spent whole nights on a regular basis. Ketchum and Roach had also visited Kitty's house on their arrival in town, he'd learned.

Jackson found the madam edgy, but keen to offer accommodations of a sort.

She pulled back the thick red curtains at her front parlour's windows. Morning light revealed dancing motes of dust and a decadence tending to shabbiness. The plush furnishings exuded an intangible stale scent — of women's toiletries masking last night's sweat and other secretions.

Kitty deposited her ample curves languorously on an overstuffed, floral-patterned divan.

'Welcome to my house, Mr Farraday. Are you sure it's not one of my pretty girls you'd like to interview? I wouldn't want you to go away feeling slighted. Unsatisfied . . .'

She raised a hand to pat into place an imaginarily straying lock of the hair piled elaborately in honey-gold glory on the top of her head. She let the robe she wore over her low-cut bodice and short skirt part revealingly.

'No, Miss Malone. I think probably only your ownself can help me with the problem I have.'

'Most gracious of you, I'm sure, Mr Farraday.'

Jackson went straight to the point of his call. 'I wanted to ask you about Miss Lilian Goodnight.'

Kitty raised her painted eyebrows. 'Misfit Lil? Bluntly, I believe Mr Goodnight's child has become a cheap tramp, though uncommon handy with a gun, I allow. Now what could I tell you about her that isn't generally known?'

'Seems Miss Lilian expressed an interest in the life of the late Jimmie Sanders, who was one of your clients. And she seems to have gone missing. Vanished.'

'Not a surprise, surely?' Kitty said with a smile. 'Her movements are mostly a mystery to the community, I understand. Forgive my disinterest, but I'm more inconvenienced by the disappearance of a girl of my own — Suey-Ling.'

A gleam came to Jackson's eyes.

'Your Oriental girl? She's gone missing, too?'

Kitty nodded her brassy blonde head sadly, but failed in Jackson's eyes to give anything but the usual impression that she was plain hard.

'I'm afraid so, Mr Farraday. These girls believe in fairy tales, you know. In knights in shining armour who'll lead them to pots of gold at the end of rainbows. They run away with the first man glib enough to sell them a dream.'

'Do you think they could've gone together?' Jackson asked.

'Misfit Lil and Suey-Ling? I hadn't thought of it, but it is an idea, I suppose.'

Noting the hopeful interest in Jackson's face, she added, 'Then again, runaway girls are no great rarity, Mr Farraday. I see them all the time. Coming and going. Many are the young women who, ostracized by families and communities, attempt to start their lives over by travelling to the newer territories. Most change their names and fabricate new backgrounds. It makes a girl — or even two together — impossible to trace.'

Kitty's warning had the ring of truth. She was telling him what a seasoned frontiersman already knew. He stroked his chin beard absently.

It was easy to disappear. New identities were easy to establish, but difficult to prove since official records, such as birth certificates and marriage licences, didn't exist or were conveniently lost, especially in undeveloped Western communities. Photography, as a form of identification, was not yet popular or widespread.

Kitty said ingenuously, 'I do like your cut, Mr Farraday. You're a resourceful man who cares, but I really can't answer your questions.'

A smile touched her lips that wasn't wholly professional.

'Maybe you could let me help you some other way,' she said. 'A little relief from the burden of your worries perhaps. A distracting treat from myself or an engagement with an attentive girl of your choice . . . '

Jackson felt his cheeks crimson hotly under their weathered bronze.

'Generous and delightful, I'm sure, but it won't be necessary, Miss Malone,' he said roughly. 'I've intruded here long enough.'

'Oh,' Kitty said, face falling in disappointment. 'Is there nothing I can do for you?'

It was an offer Jackson realized he could turn to better purpose than anything the madam envisaged.

8

LAME DUCK SHERIFF

Lil had a vague sense of being wrapped and bound in a blanket and being swung to and fro like a human sausage. The swaying feeling and the shape of her predicament somehow reminded her of Flash Sam Whittaker standing up in his bathtub with everything showing; of Kitty setting him in motion.

She tried to wriggle, she tried to see, but could do neither.

Her head swam and she felt sick. She could draw scarcely enough rasping breath though her wind-pipe, which was sore and swollen. In entering the gaming boss's sanctum, she'd taken a tiger by the tail. Restrained in the enveloping blanket, she was in for the ride — wherever it was taking her, however it would end.

Dimly, in consciousness that returned to her in fits and starts, like the unwinding spring of a faulty clock, she guessed at her fate — maybe she'd be buried alive, or thrown into a lake or river . . .

Broken time ticked by. Panic bubbled up during one of her murky mind's clearer moments. She figured she was being transported in a jolting wagon. Desperately, she tried wriggling again.

A voice far-off said, 'Lie still, you stupid bitch! You'll be taken someplace a long ways off . . . where you can't cause trouble, but where they can use a young female like you. You got a firm, healthy body under those men's duds. Make more nuisance of yourself and you won't get even that chance!'

It wasn't Flash Sam who spoke, but it was a voice she vaguely recognized. Whose . . . ?

The only comfort Lil could draw from her predicament was that she wasn't slated to die yet. Another bump, a glancing blow to her head. Her depressing thoughts span away again, back into the black pain, then into nothingness.

★ ★ ★

'Sheriff Hamish Howard? I must confess I hadn't given him a thought.'

'Why not, Miss Malone?' Jackson Farraday asked. 'He is the law here. Maybe he could wire descriptions to fellow officers in other townships. The girls have to be somehere.'

Kitty Malone's smile held an amused malice. 'Well, you must be the first person I've heard to cast Sheriff Howard in the role of a detective! His talent generally runs more in the direction of managing the county purse.'

'Can't do harm for the two of us to report the girls missing and ask for some action,' Jackson said.

It struck him ruefully that she was probably right. He couldn't himself imagine Hamish Howard eagerly getting off his ass to set inquiries in train about two girls of dubious character.

One was a notorious pest; the other — not to put too fine a point on it — a prostitute of non-Anglo-Saxon race.

Kitty made play at studying on the proposition.

'Yes, I expect you're right . . . the — er — forces of law and order should be properly enlisted.'

Jackson couldn't tell if she was making fun of him or the sheriff, but he was glad when she said she'd fetch her coat and bonnet.

Jackson set on his own hat and stepped to the door. He was glad to leave the cloying fustiness of Kitty's parlour and breathe fresh air.

The sheriff regarded Jackson's return to his office with intense suspicion. His small eyes were unhappy, and very wary. 'Not more dead outlaws, I hope,' he said.

'Oh, no, Sheriff,' Kitty said. 'This is a different tale of woe.'

It puzzled Jackson that the madam could put on lightheartedness. Evidently, she wasn't as anxious as he to find the missing girls, but he guessed hardness about suchlike came easily to a woman who ran a house of ill repute.

He explained the nature of their business. 'The girls could've been taken way forcibly, against their wishes. Abducted,' he finished.

Howard couldn't or didn't want to believe the suggestion. He was scathing.

'Jest supposin' we know how an' which way they went an' can find tracks, where do I raise a posse to run down the abductors of a China woman and a delinquent brat disowned by her own parent?'

Kitty said, 'I feel it in my bones. We've seen the last of them, Mr Farraday. Runaway girls like Suey-Ling aren't unheard of, and I fear that without the protection of a good household, such as my own — without roots or family — they do come to unpleasant ends.'

Howard nodded sagely and more vigorously than he did for most information. Jackson could see how it was — the pair of them were in cahoots, ganging up to reject his entreaties.

'Indians, Negroes, Chinese . . . they're fair game, ain't they?' Howard said, winking.

The lazy sheriff reflected the social attitude of the time, which made out the non-white girl was naturally immoral and which equated prostitution with a status of human inferiority. Jackson didn't accept this. He was out of step in his thinking on what in respectable circles was either ignored or actively crusaded against.

To Jackson, all women were creatures whose nature was largely a mystery. In point of fact, he reckoned he didn't care for any female temperament. But prostitution — not a well-understood phenomenon at all — filled a need in the West. Men largely outnumbered women and wives were therefore not easily found.

He made a last appeal to Kitty.

'Intuition aside, ma'am, don't you

think we owe it to the girls to look for 'em, however hopeless the case?'

She made a tired gesture. 'I pay the taxes for my house and my girls, Mr Farraday. The sheriff here knows that and on his own admission, he's in no position to look into the matter. We'll have to let it rest. I'm sorry.'

'I'm sorry, too,' Jackson said.

But he concluded Kitty Malone, though curiously strained, was in no way distressed. By 'paying her taxes', like Flash Sam Whittaker and an influential few other voters, she effectively bought off the law in Silver Vein. Howard trotted around doing their errands and turning a blind eye, and they were given a free hand in whatever swindles they cared to mount.

Kitty's initial scorn and her smug co-operation in Howard's indolence suggested to Jackson she might not want the girls found, and he wondered why.

He escorted her back to the boarding house, thinking to question her further.

She was by no means reluctant to entertain, and offered him refreshment.

'Why don't you come in again, Jackson — if I may call you that as a friend? Perhaps you would take some tea, or something a little exciting . . . chocolate, champagne?'

Jackson accepted the invitation to go in, determined she should disclose to him all she knew about Suey-Ling.

He was returned to the close, perfumed atmosphere of the front parlour. Kitty excused herself momentarily to change from her outdoor clothes. She came back to recline herself again on the sofa, propping her feet on a foot-stool.

Jackson drew a deep breath and plunged with a point-blank question. 'Were Suey-Ling and Misfit Lil known to one another?'

'I believe they did keep company from time to time,' Kitty murmured languidly. 'Haven't you bothered yourself enough with such tiresome matters? Your duty has been fulfilled most admirably in that respect . . . '

She settled herself back further and once more let the robe inch open. Jackson saw she'd not only divested herself of cloak and bonnet, but bodice and skirt to boot. He caught glimpses of pink flesh, a flimsy chemise and loose-fitting drawers.

'But where do you think they might've gone? To Salt Lake City? Down the Old Spanish Trail?'

'Do help me let you forget it, Jackson!'

'But I can't,' he said simply.

Suddenly, Kitty bent down in great apparent pain and pulled up the robe to rub the calf of her right leg.

'Oh, ah, aah! Cramp . . . The torture of it! Here — rub my leg!'

The robe gaped.

Jackson got to his feet — not to do as she asked but to turn from the exposure of not just shapely legs, but a heaving bosom and drawers that, open at the slit, exposed a bush of curly brown hair and more. He was no prude, but the tactics she was employing to avoid answering his questions made clear he wasn't going to learn anything from her he couldn't learn from any whore.

He could think of only one other person who might be able to tell him more about Misfit Lil and Suey-Ling's disappearance.

As he wrenched open the parlour door and strode out into the front passage for the door, he heard Kitty laugh jerkily.

'Why, Mr Farraday! A fine, mature man like you, and scared of a woman's body!'

But the colour had drained from her face, leaving the raw bitterness of rage and frustration. She'd failed to divert him.

Leaving the house, Jackson heard her spit viciously, 'Goddamn it!'

★ ★ ★

Indian Bureau agent Claude J. Frenzeny headed for the reservation in the black-leather, upholstered driving seat of a light spring wagon well loaded with a mixed cargo from a freight warehouse in Silver Vein.

In the wagon's tray were kegs of bolts and nails, several sets of mail-order farming implements, groceries including canned grub like sardines in tomato sauce and peaches — which were delicacies for himself — a roll of heavy tarpaulin, and two other, more mysterious rolls of what looked like old blanket bound up with rope, but which produced occasional noises and odd writhings.

Frenzeny was no stranger to fishy business. He'd built up a life in the territory on duplicity, but it had never previously included what amounted to abduction and whoremongering. He had misgivings but, always attentive to his private luxuries, he wondered what might lie for him personally in the latest piece of dirty dealing.

Every so often he'd slash the hindquarters of his team with a whip and idly curse the beasts, after which they would trot for a minute or two before reverting to their deliberate, plodding pace. He had plenty of time to dwell on his past and future, if not intentionally.

Frenzeny had been reared in a merchant-class household in New Orleans, Louisiana. His family was of the *ancienne population*, tracing its ancestry back to the French and Spanish colonial periods. His grandfather and father had participated in the great steamboat trade which had begun on the Mississippi River in 1812 and by 1830 had made New Orleans the nation's busiest export hub. But after the 1850s, the family had fallen on difficult times. Railroads had diverted the valley's commerce to an east-west axis, silt affected the waterways, and a heady era was over, at least for the Frenzenys.

Young Claude envied the people who still had the money he should have had; people of quality, like himself, who were able to observe gracious conventions in a city with a European cultural heritage. Denied a career in commerce, he flirted for a time with the idea of being a chemist.

He also found time to flirt with the wife of a chemistry professor. Till a duel was mooted . . . Then Claude Frenzeny left town in a hurry. Speaking plain, the bored wife had never been of any use beyond available amusement for a young man who possessed neither money nor natural charm to attract the opposite sex. She was no great beauty and was marked by the coarseness and appetite of years more advanced than his own.

His best option had been to follow the great American dream that was moving westward. He came to the frontier. It was a dog-eat-dog place, and to that extent Frenzeny discovered he was in his element. Sharp business practice was in his blood.

Old family contacts and his own good opinion of himself had won him the patronage of an obscure religious sect. Fortuitously for Frenzeny at this difficult time, the Secretary of the Interior had extended the concept of civil, religious administration to cover the whole Indian Bureau. Agencies were distributed among Christian denominations on the basis of missionary work done among the respective tribes. Boosted by his repute as a 'churchman', flimsy though it was, Frenzeny got himself nominated as an agent. The salary was meagre, but the position, in a part of the West far from Washington's overview, opened up opportunities for all manner of venal trading and corruption.

In high places, later decisions were made and new policies formed, but on the ground change was implemented only slowly. Frenzeny thought he had it made. He continued to cheat his charges and divert funds for the shelter and safe passage of outlaws riding the trail that eventually led to the Mexican border.

Innocent settlers were terrorized and run off by renegades from the reservation. Cattle were rustled by the incoming white riff-raff, switched, rebranded and driven to the holding pens of fellow traders — criminals — in distant towns.

It was a fine scheme, except that final control had to be vested in hands more powerful and ruthless than his own; the shadowy king-rats of LOOO. Which was why he found himself foisted with the chore of disposing of two young females who, surprising though it seemed, had managed to become a nuisance to the powerful organization.

In frustration, he took another crack of the whip at his horses. The pair lunged against the harness. A rattling run broke the rhythmic clop of their hoofs.

Frenzeny leaned against the seat-back of the lurching wagon. Behind him, one of the blanket rolls wriggled frantically.

'Quit your fretting, kid!' he snapped

over his shoulder. 'You trying to make that blanket a shroud?'

The simplest, safest course would be to kill the girls and destroy or hide their bodies. Yet Frenzeny baulked at this. He'd have to very careful. People didn't take kindly to women being killed, a prohibition that went as far as to include soiled doves. Also, he didn't know whether he was capable of killing two young women in cold blood, and it would be such a waste.

His eye was always to trade, to making a profit, and he knew a handsome profit awaited young female flesh if it could be transported south to the eager bordellos of Old Mexico. The China doll and the lively *norteamericano* filly would be prized by the populace there, both local and fugitive.

Here, of course, though not typical, was just another trading situation to be properly exploited.

And before that, it would be fun to taste the wares himself. Frenzeny liked to think himself a cut above average, but women didn't exactly fall at his feet. When he was without his derby hat and his concealing, outsize store suit, he had to concede regretfully what his mirror told him. He looked bloated, his skin was pallid and his belly inclined to flabbiness. It was a long while since he'd had the opportunity to bed a young woman.

Hell, it was high time he changed that. Maybe this problem could be turned into his lucky day.

9

ONE FALSE MOVE . . .

It was uncomfortably hot within the tight wrapping of blanket and Misfit Lil was thirsty and hungry, but she refused to be panicked and willed an icy calm to settle itself over her. She was probably closer to death than she'd ever been. Struggle, as her captor had warned, would only worsen her situation. Now, what she had to do was wait and be ready when the time came for action. If it did . . .

She knew this country like the palm of her hand; its sounds like the melody of a favourite song. She calculated from the vibrations of the wagon in which she was conveyed that they were travelling into the canyonlands on an ascending trail south-west of Silver Vein. She made shrewd guesses at their destination but didn't want to be so bold as to give them certain name.

She also thought she could give a name at last to the man who growled at her and called her a silly bitch.

The wagon began to slow again and this time the driver didn't use his cracking whip to stir the horses into a faster gait. Maybe they'd almost arrived at wherever they were going — an isolated spot for sure — and the time must be drawing nigh when she'd have the chance to fight for her life.

The wagon took a sharp turn to the left. Lil rolled in her blanket, unable to do anything about it. She uttered a ripe but muffled curse. The jolting increased and the wagon proceeded on an angle of steep descent.

She thought, 'My guesswork's right. I know where I am even though I'm virtually blindfolded.'

Final confirmation came from a sound and a smell. The sound, though a little distant and deadened by blanket, could only be described as a woofing or grunting. The smell was musky, skunk-like.

Misfit Lil knew exactly what wild animals made the sound and the distinctive smell, noticeable over hundreds of feet. Their habitat was desert and dry woodlands. Especially and vitally, a herd would congregate in the shade of bushes in a canyon which had plenty of waterholes. And Lil knew of one place in particular in her country where a group of the unlovely beasts had marked out such a territory with the scent glands on their hairy rumps.

Javelina Bend!

The crooked Indian agent Claude Frenzeny — for his had to be the voice she'd finally placed — was taking her to the big log cabin dignified with the title of reservation sub-office.

The solid but primitive building was close by the stage road to Silver Vein. The nearest Apache dwellings were two miles distant, up into some concealing hills. The sub-office was located at Javelina Bend allegedly for the easy collection of mail delivered by passing coaches.

The reason was a farcical fabrication, Lil reminded herself scornfully, since the mail consisted largely of bureau memoranda from Washington and Frenzeny had no intention of complying with them. More likely, the cabin gave him a convenient place to rendezvous with men going down the Outlaw Trail. She'd observed him doing shady business with dyed-in-the-wool ruffians of every stripe, assorted drifters escaping monotony and cowboys turned bad for one reason or another.

The wagon was brought to a halt. Soon, Lil thought, it would be time to act. Then or never . . .

She heard Frenzeny climb down from the wagon seat and walk around to the rear.

'I'm going to cut you loose, Lil Goodnight,' he said. 'You and the China whore. When you're ready, you can get down and walk to the cabin you'll see. But hear this — I'll have a gun levelled at you all the time. One false move and life'll be over for you in a wink. No skin offa my nose, slut.'

Lil heard the opening of a clasp-knife and the cutting of cords. Though her limbs were stiff and cramped, she was able to shrug herself out of the enveloping roll of blanket and sit up.

Blinking against the strength of the sunlight, she saw all her guesses were right. The wagon, with reins wound around the seat-brace, was outside the Javelina Bend sub-office.

Over its closed door she could see the carved plaque which she knew was inscribed, hypocritically in view of Frenzeny's abuse of his responsibilities to the Indians, 'Let your light so shine before men, that they may see your good works, and glorify your Father which is in heaven.'

She took several deep, gulping breaths through her bruised throat.

'Claude Frenzeny!' she croaked. 'I knew it. You're in cahoots with Flash Sam Whittaker, aren't you? The Injun unrest, the gunrunning, the beef racket, the cattle rustling. They're all parts of the same nasty game. Fine Christian missionary you turn out to be . . . 'good works', your creole momma's stinking ass!'

Her rasping voice forced the words out in snarling contempt. With no other weapon, this was mind against mind, and she thought she had Frenzeny's measure. Her accusations hit the mark as neatly as she could have put bullets through the pips on a playing card.

They had precisely the effect on the prideful Frenzeny that she intended.

'I'm a respected servant of government and community,' he claimed, arrogant but stung.

She goaded him some more. 'Huh! Them peace policy initiatives have never had a chance to work. Trash like you have seen to that. The system's corrupt, a sham, designed for feathering the nests of humbugs and frauds. How else do you spend twice over your $1,500 salary?'

'You're a nobody!' he burst out. 'A cheap female tramp, handy with a gun . . . consorting with alien whores!'

'Yeah, at least they'll talk to me,' she retorted. 'You, they wouldn't give time of day. Triple pay wouldn't get you a roll in the filthiest crib, you slimy, hypocritical toad!'

For a fact, she couldn't see the middle-aged, oily Frenzeny being the object of any girl's affections. He was lazy and had crafty but lecherous eyes. The impression she'd had so many times before was reinforced: under his oddly citified dress and air of moral superiority, he was rotten to the core. She knew he took the food out the Indians' mouths and dickered over it with outlaws to make a profit that went into his own pocket. Her friend, the scout Jackson Farraday, had explained how it might be done.

'Shut your trap, woman!' he snapped back at her. 'Who do you think you are? You seem to be forgetting your life's in — '

'Your dirty hands,' she completed, talking over him. 'But you're forgetting what I know I am. I'm Misfit Lil.'

He laughed triumphantly yet shakily. 'But you ain't got your guns!' He sneered. 'Princess of Pistoleers! Your rep doesn't spook me.'

'No? But you have to hold a gun on me.' She smiled mockingly. 'I'd say you were scared.'

'That ain't scared. Just careful. Curb your tongue, missy, or where you're going it'll be the first thing that'll get cut out!'

Suey-Ling, whom he'd also released from her blanket binding, was sitting up. She moaned and said something in her own lingo. Either her powers of recuperation were lesser than Lil's or she'd been drugged. The pupils of her almond-shaped eyes were black and dilated. A heavy dose of laudanum?

'Look what your fine partners have done to that poor unfortunate,' Lil said. 'It's outrageous.'

Frenzeny's attention momentarily

shifted to the other girl.

'You shouldn't have spoken to her, used her name at the El Dorado. Come on, get down out of there, the both of you!' he ordered. 'I want you in the cabin, then we'll see who's boss around here. You'll get your first lessons in doing what you're told and liking it. Think on this — from now on, if you want life at all there's gonna be men in it who'll be less gentle than me!'

He reached for Suey-Ling, the smaller of the two girls, and with one hand dragged her over the wagon's opened tailgate. Limp and unresisting, she fell aheap into the dust.

'Aaaah . . .'

Lil, meanwhile, eased herself to the edge of the tray and lowered one leg so her foot was on the ground. As she slipped the rest of her body's weight on to it, Frenzeny clutched Suey-Ling's high collar to haul her to her unsteady legs.

Lil made her move. She stumbled

deliberately and fell heavily against Frenzeny.

The paunchy man lost his balance. He ripped out a shattering, livid oath, most blasphemous for a churchman, and sat down heavily on his fat backside.

Lil fell on top of him. Before he could bring the menacing revolver to bear, Lil jabbed her bunched knuckles into the softness of his belly like a piston. The punch drove the foul wind out of him in a gasping, tortured wheeze. His face went the colour of dirty alkali.

She was about to chop at his arm and make a grab for the gun when suddenly, from the tail of her eye, she saw the cabin's door swing open.

Two roughnecks spilled out from the low building which she'd supposed was empty. Alerted by Frenzeny's cry, they came at a run.

Lil cursed. A last, unexpected turn of the cards had gone against her. No time now to get the revolver. Or was there?

Frenzeny was struggling for breath and the approaching men hadn't yet drawn the guns they wore in tied-down holsters low on their hips.

In that tense second, Lil rolled like a scalded wild-cat, then sprang up from knees and elbows. She kicked hard at Frenzeny's gun hand and the weapon span high from his grip, clattering into nearby rocks.

Frenzeny screeched.

Lil's effort had made her weak and dizzy, but she knew that with her plan miscarrying, she had to run for her life. If she was lucky, maybe she could still get Frenzeny's gun before the two roughnecks could be told what was going on and bring their weapons into play.

She fixed a glitter of sun on metal in the rocks. She pounced for it.

Frenzeny, his breath partially regained and his white face set in vicious lines of fury, yelled, 'It's Misfit Lil! Shoot the bitch . . . don't let her get away!'

Lil's pounce became a scrambling

dive. The roughnecks' pistols crashed, once, twice. Slugs whistled over her head and screamed shatteringly off rock.

But her hands were on the Colt and she scooped it up and swung round, firing as she did so.

For a snap shot made on the move, it was good enough. She hit no one, but it gave Frenzeny and his two associates, plunging across the open hardpack in front of the cabin, reason to seek cover behind the wagon.

'You won't get away, slut!' Frenzeny bawled. 'There's nowhere out here for you to run. We got horses and you haven't. Give yourself up, or we'll hunt you down like game!'

Ducked down behind the rocks, Lil said, 'I think not, Frenzeny. If I want to disappear into the canyons, I can.'

Lil checked the cylinder of the seized gun. Only four shots remained of the Colt's load. It was bad news but no worse than she'd expected. She had no other ammunition on her, and four cartridges weren't enough to shoot the issue out safely, even if she was the redoubtable Misfit Lil. She had no inflated ideas about her skills. She knew she wasn't that invincible.

For maybe the count of three the picture held. Was it a standoff? An impasse?

Mad with rage, Frenzeny again told the low-life renegades who'd been staying over in the agency cabin to shoot her down.

'Fill the goddamn bitch with lead, boys, and I'll give you the China floozy for dessert!'

The pair peered over the wagon. They jockeyed and bobbed up time and again to let loose a volley of shots in Misfit Lil's direction.

The roar of gunshots filled the air, echoing up and down the canyon. Rock splinters and dust flew.

Much as it galled Lil to make no reply, she kept her head down and backed off, weaving her supple body at ground level through the jumble of boulders. Being outnumbered, she determined not to fire back a single shot that wasn't a cast-iron certainty to better her predicament.

Moreover, she had no intention of leaving Suey-Ling to suffer the trio's evil designs. When the time was ripe, she'd free the pretty young Oriental from their clutches. To succeed, she'd have to keep every bullet she had and make it count.

When she reached the right spot, she tucked the Colt in her waistband and retreated on light feet into the buckled, brown and ochre citadels of an area where erosion had created weird rock formations that provided a maze of natural escape routes. To those without knowledge, it was some of the most forbidding and desolate country in the territory. To Lil, it was a place of refuge.

She leaped from rock to rock in a series of long-legged strides, never dislodging loose stuff and staying doubled over, covering a lot of ground quickly and quietly, like she'd seen the Indians do.

Heat made the cruel landscape shimmer and warned Lil she needed to get to water and proper shade. Soon, in a weakened state from her captivity and the ordeal of travel in Frenzeny's wagon, she'd probably lose control of her senses and her limbs unless she rested up.

★   ★   ★

Frenzeny and the others eventually came forward cautiously, hoping to find Misfit Lil's riddled body among the tumbled rocks. None of them liked taking the risk.

'The loco dove's got your gun, Claude,' the surlier of the hardcases reminded. 'Why the hell did yuh bring the spitfire here?'

Exasperated, Frenzeny said, 'It was LOOO orders. I had no choice, 'cept to've bashed the girls to death maybe and dumped the bodies, which seemed at the time like a pure tragedy.'

It took the three a long, fretful

interval to search a square mile of the rugged slopes, aware every moment that one if not more of them could be shot to death from ambush.

'There should be a sign here saying 'Proceed at own peril',' the surly man said.

But nothing moved except the quivering heat-waves. By the time they finally acknowledged Lil had disappeared into the arid maze, Frenzeny was in a frenzy.

His teeth showed in a devil's snarl. 'I should've made Misfit Lil buzzard bait while I had the chance,' he conceded. 'But this thing ain't over yet . . . '

10

SUNDOWN'S SECRETS

Jackson Farraday left Kitty Malone's knowing he'd exhausted avenues of inquiry in Silver Vein. Sheriff Hamish Howard was unmoved by the disappearance of Misfit Lil and Suey-Ling, and Kitty was intent only on diverting him from a mystery that seemed to be of concern to himself alone.

Those citizens of a persuasion to be scandalized were still gossiping and conjecturing about the shooting deaths of Jimmie Sanders and a pair of wanted gunnies from other parts. Two missing girls of no high repute were seldom mentioned, although the odd biddy could occasionally be overheard muttering on the dusty streets and walks the likes of 'Good riddance to the young trollops.'

The other item of mild interest in

town was that Doc Smithers had been called to the El Dorado to attend to employee Burt Ireland. They said he'd fallen down the backstairs, breaking an arm and a leg and injuring his neck.

No one seemed able to account for the accident to Flash Sam's burliest bully-boy. A niggle at the back of Jackson's mind told him it bore scrutiny, but its apparent irrelevance to the matter in hand, plus the unapproachability of Flash Sam, who regarded the behind-the-scenes operations of his gambling house as confidential, obliged him to put it aside.

The finding of Misfit Lil, whether or not the alleged absconding of Kitty's Oriental girl was connected, was paramount.

Frankly, Lilian Goodnight could be the pest Lieutenant Michael Covington trenchantly maintained. She was inclined to be raucous and passionate when she made a stand. She was driven as much by impulse as reason. But Jackson appreciated her sense of humour, manifested in an irony ranging from incisive to gentle, and her youthfulness that lingered in a sweetness hard to define.

At bottom, young Miss Lilian was tough even to self-destructiveness, yet warm-hearted in the way only a woman could be. He could fleetingly wish he was ten years younger, in which case he would have had no compunction about taking advantage of her unwarranted hero-worship of himself. As always, he found it cause for regret that she and Mike Covington didn't hit it off. Each was exactly what the other needed, he believed.

He also believed Covington, and Fort Dennis, would have no interest in finding out what had become of Lil, if anything. Since her return from Boston, she'd made a disconcerting habit of popping up at any point of the compass. Her present absence from obvious haunts wouldn't be taken as serious cause for alarm. Which left solving the puzzle up to himself.

Jackson had a sneaking and growing

suspicion that part of the answer lay at the source of the question: with Sundown Sanders.

He saddled up his sorrel at the livery barn and settled the bronc to a steady but urgent pace on the road to the Diamond S horse ranch.

Arriving, he rode up to the ranch-house. He noted the long-established orderliness of the spread, but also signs of patch and repair that suggested not much new money had been spent in a while. It also struck him that the place was no longer crewed by employed hands, which also told a story, of course.

He was reminded that rumour had it Sundown Sanders had felt obliged to cover his son's gambling debts at the El Dorado and they'd been to a grand tune, which might not have been entirely disclosed.

He dismounted and let the reins drag. The sorrel would wait obediently and at the ready.

The aroma and sizzle of bacon in a

frying-pan reached him on the porch steps. He rapped on the door.

'I seed an' heared yuh, Jackson Farraday!' Sundown called. 'Come on in.'

Crouched by a blackened grille over the fireplace, the old man turned his slices of bacon with a long fork and kept an eye on a bubbling pot of beans. Coffee simmered alongside the glowing logs in another pot.

His face was etched with deep worry lines in the red firelight. 'What is it, Jackson?' he asked. 'Is it about Misfit Lil?'

'I'll say it is,' Jackson said without preliminary. 'You figured she might run into some kinda danger. I reckon she has.'

He gave a brisk, matter-of-fact report, just like he was reporting to Colonel Lexborough on a scouting mission. He left out the details of Kitty's attempted seduction, not seeing yet how it fitted into the scheme of things, if at all.

As he listened, Sundown's sombre expression changed. By the time Jackson finished, he looked agitated and ashamed.

'I never wanted no more murders on my head, goddamn it!' he blurted in wild distress. 'Do yuh think the gals is kilt?'

'I don't know,' Jackson said, gravely and honestly. 'I hope not, but to find out, I'll need more facts to follow up. And I've been doing some studying on that. This began with Jimmie's troubles. I'm not sure you've given out the kit-and-caboodle of them. You want to tell more?'

The accusation made the old man stiffen. Silently, he pulled the pan of crackling bacon off the fire, straightened up and tottered to a shelf, from where he lifted a bottle of whiskey.

He said, 'Guess I got no choice no more, if'n it'll give yuh a chance to find them gals. An' it can't hurt Jimmie — only his mem'ry and fam'ly pride. I hate to say it, Jackson, but yuh're right.

I ain't been plumb straight.'

He slopped coffee into a tin mug and handed another to Jackson. 'Help yuhself.'

To his own mug, he added a generous slug of gurgling liquor before passing the whiskey bottle to Jackson. He downed half his doctored coffee at a gulp.

Jackson poured, sipped and waited patiently. The coffee was hot, black and sugarless. He didn't lace it with the whiskey. Maybe he was going to need a very clear head.

In a choked voice, Sundown began his story.

'Jimmie's downfall weren't no card-playin', though that were bad 'nough. It were women — or mebbe I should make that one woman in pertikler . . . '

'I can guess,' Jackson said, nodding. 'Kitty Malone.'

'Yuh got it, mister!' Sundown growled. 'I figger she led him on some, like he was the only man she cared for. Jimmie were blind to the fact she were only a cat-house madam. Howsumever, like a damn fool I kept m' 'pinions to m' ownself. By the time I found out the racket she were leadin' him into, it were too late. Jimmie had gotten kinda — besotted.'

Sundown laughed in a brittle way and gulped the rest of his fumy coffee. 'Weren't apt to lissen to no reason from his own pa after a whiles. Waal, he were a grown man, I figgered. Had to make his own mistakes — l'arn fer hisself — find out thar's considerable more to a designin' woman than big tits an' a gen'rous ass. An' to my lastin' regret, I let him get on playin' with fire.'

The look in the old-timer's eyes was that more usually seen in the eyes of guilty, hunted men than in the eyes of a bereaved father.

'I couldn't say it didn't matter to me an' mean it,' the anguished man confessed, his haunted eyes filling up. 'He were his dead ma's boy . . . my Jilly's. They was cut'n offa the same bolt.'

Wise in the ways of human nature as he was in many other things, Jackson could understand how a man might love a son no matter how he acted; no matter how distant or withdrawn he became. He probed, gently.

'So how was it Jimmie offended? What was it Kitty Malone got Jimmie to do?'

Sundown wiped the back of a hand across his whiskery face, pulled himself together and got back on track.

'Kitty never wanted no golden ring offa Jimmie like he tried to fool hisself. She were a whore, doin' it fer money. Or mebbe when it started, she wanted someone fresh to play with. Only a numbskull could b'lieve she ever did love him anyways. But what she ended up sellin' him were a bill o' goods fer sure. Damn her black soul!'

Jackson could see the old man was straying, too mortified to come to the point. He hunched up his shoulders in bewilderment, although the glimmering of a startling explanation for all kinds of skull-duggery was beginning to form in his mind.

'Tell me then — Kitty fooled him how?'

'Her story went the gals' boardin' house was mortgaged to Flash Sam, which were true 'nough, I guess. She said she had to pay off the debt to Sam — get the house back — afore she could sell up the sorry consarn an' clear out clean to Denver with Jimmie. She swore she wanted to be Jimmie's wife an' this were the only way.'

'And Jimmie swallowed it?' Jackson prompted.

'The whole passel o' lies.' Sundown sighed. 'Have us some more whiskey?'

Jackson refrained from saying he hadn't had any yet, but his lack of response didn't stop Sundown tossing back another half a mug.

'Seems Flash Sam needed a job done fer crim'nal pals in the North-east,' Sundown went on, his bleary eyes watering anew. 'Kitty said if she could fix it fer Sam, she'd get back her house

154

deeds in payment.'

'What was the job?' Jackson asked, hardly daring to voice his guess.

'Certain parties wanted — stuff — run to them red murderers in the canyonlands an' mountains, Angry-fist an' his reservation jumpers.'

'By stuff you mean guns,' Jackson said sternly.

Blusteringly, Sundown tried to defend the indefensible. 'Most times I reck'n Jimmie jest couldn't see no evil in what they was doin'! My boy were given to seein' the best in ever'body anyways. It's howcome he fell head over heels for that Jezebel in the first place. I swear he were lost from then on in. He couldn't back out . . . '

Jackson could piece together for himself more of the links that would flesh out Sundown's disjointed revelations. It was the gullible Jimmie who freighted weapons to the hostiles, no doubt using a string of the reliable Diamond S pack-ponies — surefooted animals descended from Indian herds.

155

They were strong but smaller than fourteen hands high at the withers, and the Sanders ranch specially bred and trained them for work in the mountains.

He said harshly, 'You should have told me this before, after Jimmie was killed. Maybe told Misfit Lil, too.'

Sundown looked at Jackson pleadingly, conscious now of bitter and abject shame. 'I didn't want the whole o' Silver Vein to know.'

'Hell, would it have mattered? Angry-fist's raiders have brought death and destruction to this country with contraband guns. Now two innocent girls might also be dead! And how-come Jimmie had to die? Did he steal the gunrunners' dirty money?'

'Naw! He never handled no money,' Sundown protested. 'Kitty were two-timin'. She dumped Jimmie an' it broke him up. He still couldn't see she were jest low-down, gutter trash. She'd p'isined his brain. He didn't want to live no more. It'd hit him that hard.

Next thing the gunnies showed, an' Jimmie let 'em kill him! That's how-come it happened.'

Still, why had the executioners come looking for Jimmie Sanders in the first place?

Jackson didn't know or care just then. All he cared about was that Flash Sam Whittaker stood accused on Sundown's testimony as the local kingpin of a far-flung crime syndicate, and Kitty Malone was up to her smooth neck in its affairs, too. It confirmed his creed that the more voluptuous a woman, the less she was to be trusted, he told himself darkly. He was ready to bet that, between them, Kitty and Flash Sam had the answers to the disappear-ance of Misfit Lil and Suey-Ling.

Maybe they'd done away with the girls as ruthlessly as Jimmie Sanders had been eliminated. His blood boiled at the thought. He was raring to go.

'This is all bad news, Sundown, you must know that,' he said. 'I'm sorry it looks like Jimmie was double-crossed, but he did wrong and I've no time to waste commiserating. I've got to get back to Silver Vein, pronto.'

He had a vague but as yet hasty notion of facing the boss of the town's rackets and his immoral consort; of challenging them with Sundown's charges.

He went out, lifted into the saddle, jerked the sorrel's head around and urged it into a canter.

11

TICKET TO HELL

The town lazed in the afternoon sun, presenting a front of orderly, quiet respectability. A few older men lounged against the wall of McHendry's saloon on the wide wooden sidewalk, nothing questionable about them beyond idleness. A couple of bonneted ladies with parasols chatted outside Goldberg's emporium.

Despite the prevailing calm, so out of step with his own sense of urgency, Jackson Farraday felt that beneath a deceptive surface, affairs were coming to a boil in the town. Surely a lid couldn't much longer be kept on the links between Indian troubles, gunrunning, cattle-rustling, the assassination of Jimmie Sanders, the possible kidnapping of Lilian Goodnight and Suey-Ling, and the machinations of

Flash Sam Whittaker.

He was tempted to take Sundown Sanders's revelations to Fort Dennis, but he feared this would cause delay that might be fatal to the missing girls if they still lived. Lieutenant Covington would need to be persuaded; Colonel Lexborough would be cautious, reluctant to involve the military in ostensibly civil matters. The Indian unrest was in Jackson's mind a plain product of white men's incitement, but he had yet to find proof that would meet the Army's, and possibly political, satisfaction.

Acceptable proof — some evidence — might be at the El Dorado. Could the two girls be held there captive? Single-handed, could he beat the truth out of Whittaker and Malone?

No. The heavily muscled numbers of Flash Sam's guards would be against him.

He considered and quickly dismissed calling on the Sheriff's Office. Hamish Howard was a Whittaker man, of course. Flash Sam had to have him under his control to operate his raft of dubious activities, especially the El Dorado.

The sorrel carried him past Kitty Malone's boarding house where not only each red curtain but every dusty window was closed. The place looked dead, Jackson thought absently. It was not until he came to the El Dorado that formless disquiet blossomed into huge unease. Between the imposing Grecian columns, the heavy doors were shut and barred.

Jackson swung down. He hitched the sorrel and walked over. A fresh-looking notice had been tacked up: 'Closed until further notice. All enquiries to South Pass City Bank, Wyoming.'

Shocked, he turned from the steps uncertain what his next move should be.

One of the loafers from outside McHendry's came down the street. He called across, 'The gamblin' hall's closed. They gone — ev'ry man jack of 'em. Mebbe it ain't no bad thing!'

'When did this happen?' Jackson demanded.

The loafer shrugged. 'One, two hours back. Sudden like. Flash Sam left on the noonday stage north.' He chuckled conspiratorially. 'The whorehouse madam, Kitty Malone, shut up shop an' lit out with him. All his bully-boys saddled up an' quit town likewise. Figger they gone to greener pastures.'

Jackson's heart leaped, and dropped to his boots. The birds had flown! Somehow they'd seen the writing on the wall and had vamoosed while they could. Maybe their flight had been prompted by Misfit Lil's inquiries, or his own.

He mulled it over grimly. If the El Dorado crew was gone, too, Flash Sam's and Kitty Malone's plans would be next to impossible to uncover. Nor would he be likely to find out what had happened to Lil and Suey-Ling.

Ruefully, he realized the calm in Silver Vein was liable to be hiding not a coming to the boil but a coming off the boil. For long, self-accusing moments at his lack of insight, he was sunk.

Then he remembered Burt Ireland, busted up in a mysterious fall down stairs. With broken limbs, Ireland would have gone nowhere fast.

He found the burly gambling hall guard in a room back of Doc Smithers's place that served the town in lieu of a hospital.

He was strapped up — immobile as Jackson had surmised. He had a leg and an arm in splints and his neck was braced. He cursed his former employer and sidekicks.

'The rats've quit — run out on me!' the big, broken man whined. He willingly endorsed the loafer's report.

'I don't believe Flash Sam could've quit his business interests,' Jackson said. 'Who are South City Pass Bank? Is he headed for Wyoming?'

Ireland laughed bitterly. 'Nope. Wyoming's the last place Flash Sam's gonna go. The bank are a bunch of suckers and he's tricked 'em out of a mighty big bundle of *dinero* — loaned on the security of the grand El Dorado!'

Jackson noted the sarcasm. 'You mean the gambling house isn't so grand?'

With a very restricted shake of his head, Ireland said, 'Hell, no. It was a gamble its ownself and hasn't paid off.'

He explained how keeping up the house's overblown magnificence in a place like Silver Vein had eaten into the profits. Flash Sam could quit the gaming house with no loss once he had the bank's money. The bank, attracted by Silver Vein's mining prospects, had wanted to divert money from Atlantic City and South Pass City where gold deposits had been quickly exhausted.

'Whittaker was gettin' into strife besides with LOOO. So he framed Jimmie Sanders for the $5,000 that he took fer hisself. Now I figger the canny bastard's taken the bank's money and run. Mebbe he an' the boys'll start up someplace else under different names. Anyways,' he finished fretfully, 'they left me to fend fer m'self in this two-bit dump. It ain't square, mister. What am I s'posed to do fer the next six-month? What if I'm crippled fer life?'

Jackson couldn't answer, but he was more certain than ever only Whittaker or Kitty Malone would be able to reveal the fate of Misfit Lil and Suey-Ling.

'You can begin by telling me where Whittaker has gone,' he told the peeved henchman.

'They took the stage for Green River, but I'm bettin' they won't stay long. It's a railroad town, run by the Denver & Rio Grande Western Railway. They could ride tickets almost anyplace, hooking up with the Union Pacific north of Salt Lake City or with the Atchison, Topeka & Santa Fe in Colorado, which could take 'em east into Kansas through Dodge City, or south into New Mexico, through Santa Fe. Even to Mexico itself.'

A scout knew his geography and Jackson didn't need telling he had to catch up with Flash Sam and Kitty before they left Green River.

'Way I see it, I could get to Green River soon after the stage, though much after your sidekicks on horseback,' he said. 'It could stop a slew of grief if I start right away, to be at the railroad depot when they try to board their train.'

'Bring the rattlesnakes back, by God!'

'Don't know about that, but keep your shirt on,' he advised the angry invalid.

Hurriedly, he departed the medico's house. He took his sorrel to the livery, where he hired a fresh mount, a black gelding the hostler assured him had strong legs plus the lungs and stamina for a fast ride.

The straight trail to Green River, out past the flat tops of three buttes rising from the more level land, was through mostly bare and bleak country dotted with occasional trees, stunted cedars, and sage.

The powerful black lived up to the livery stable's promise and he arrived in

Green River before nightfall.

Although tempted to call in at a restaurant or saloon for refreshment, Jackson stabled the gelding and went directly to the railroad depot.

The railroad dominated the town's commerce since it was the area's major shipping point for livestock and mining equipment and supplies. The company had built an engine house, switching yards criss-crossed with iron track, and a hotel. A train was at the platform, its diamond-stack locomotive hissing.

Alarm coursed through him. It was imperative he should find his quarry before the train left, possibly taking the villains beyond reach. He went past the tower where the engineer was taking on water. He strode along the platform, dodging through heaps of baggage and freight, scanning the windows of the passenger cars.

Finally, when he was giving up hope, he came to the observation deck at the rear of the train. And there were Flash Sam Whittaker and Kitty Malone leaning on the rail. A stout leather bag, filled to bulging and secured with a small but strong-looking brass padlock, rested at their feet.

Jackson had made it by the skin of his teeth.

Two porters looked on pop-eyed and slack-jawed as he vaulted aboard. He hurled himself at Flash Sam and forced him back against the door to the car's interior. He bunched the front of the tailored burgundy frock-coat in his fists.

'You're going no place, Whittaker! You've got questions to answer back in Silver Vein!'

'My God!' Kitty shrieked. 'What is this?'

'Yeah, leggo of me, mister. We've done nothing — '

'Except murder and kidnapping and fraud!'

'This is a pail of hogwash, mister!'

'You're coming back to face charges,' Jackson rapped and swung him round. That was when two more apparent travellers appeared on the platform, approaching the train. They were members from the staff of the El Dorado — and Flash Sam saw them, too. With a desperate wrench, he loosened Jackson's hold, tearing his coat and dropping limply to his knees as the El Dorado pair came up to the open side of the deck.

'Quick, you men!' he rapped, ducking still lower and robbing Jackson of the cover his body had afforded. 'The sonofabitch attacked me. Shoot him dead!'

The men snatched six-guns from oiled holsters.

Jackson was no gunfighter. Nor could he match the gunspeed of a Misfit Lil, who made a sport of shooting.

Acting instinctively, he made his own clumsy draw, but he also aimed the toe of his boot under Flash Sam's ideally presented backside and propelled him off the deck toward his gun-handy henchmen with a mighty and savage kick.

Launched bruisingly into the air,

Flash Sam screamed. The El Dorado toughs' guns simultaneously crashed.

Projectiles met projected man. Flash Sam was dead before he hit his killers and they crashed in a heap to the ground. Great, bloody holes were ripped through the gambling boss by .44 slugs fired at close range.

Jackson covered the stunned hardcases with his gun. Both had already dropped their weapons.

'Christ!' Kitty whispered, her face ashen. 'They've killed Flash Sam.'

'Maybe he got what was coming to him, Kitty Malone,' Jackson said grimly. 'There's just one thing you can tell me to save your own miserable skin before you try other lies. Where are Misfit Lil and Suey-Ling?'

'I had nothing to do with it!' Kitty blurted, her sleek self-assurance in ruins and she looked haggard. 'They were handed over to the Indian agent to dispose of.'

'Claude Frenzeny?' Jackson asked, knowing now his guesses were right and

170

how it all fitted. 'Where did he take them?'

'To the sub-office at Javelina Bend, I think . . . ' The words came out of her like a sob. Then her stricken gaze returned to the bloody corpse of her partner in crime and lust. 'Sam Whittaker dead!'

But Jackson had neither the time nor inclination for tender words. Or to delay for explanations to the law in Green River. He whirled fast as light and grabbed up the padlocked leather bag.

'That's not yours!' Kitty managed weakly.

'Nor yours,' Jackson said in a voice that brooked no argument. 'It's evidence now.'

Keeping his gun drawn, he jumped to the tracks on the opposite side of the train to the platform. He crossed iron and loped from tie to tie till he was adjacent to the livery barn where he'd left the black.

The race wasn't over yet. He would

have to ride through the night, back to Silver Vein and out to the Indian Agency sub-office. Were the girls still at that remote place, desperately waiting for rescue? If so, how long would they be be held there?

How long would it be, Jackson asked himself, before they were killed or bundled off across borders to an unknowable fate? How long? How long? The question would burn him every galloped mile of the way through the falling night.

But he'd made a mistake in supposing Kitty's fangs were drawn.

12

WOMEN'S STRATAGEMS

The railway depot agent looked down at the telegram Kitty Malone had written and got busy tapping his key. Dot, dot, dot. Dash, dash, dash . . .

'South Pass City, Territory of Wyoming,' he read aloud.

'That's what the lady tells us. You don't have to recite it — just send it,' the Green River lawman said. 'There's a dangerous gunman on the loose with money stolen offa the poor devil the bank loaned it to. They oughta know. We can tell 'em where the robber's headed, Silver Vein, an' mebbe the bank'd like to report it to the sheriff there.'

The Green River lawman didn't want to be caught up in the matter. A messy shooting was trouble enough, and he didn't savvy the rights of it, since the witnesses' accounts were confused. This way, he could wash his hands of the whole boiling. Its origins were outside his bailiwick anyhow.

Despite the lateness of the hour, messages passed, were returned and passed again over the telegraph wires.

Faithless Kitty Malone, vindictive about the loss of the money rather than grieved over Flash Sam Whittaker's death, saw in her mind's eye the trap Jackson Farraday was riding into. She had to suppress a smile of vengeful triumph.

★ ★ ★

Misfit Lil made no idle boast that she could survive in the wilderness of the canyons. She knew the precious water-holes; the places where there was the shade of brush and where she might gather fruit and berries, capture small game perhaps.

A group of javelinas — the musk

hogs she'd smelled from Frenzeny's wagon — chose to live here. She spied on the colony and ascertained it numbered between fifteen and twenty bodies, barrel-shaped and a grizzled, dark grey with a yellowish band of bristles running under the neck. They grubbed with disc-shaped snouts, eating the grass shoots, roots, bulbs, berries, flowers, mushrooms, and fruit the habitat provided in favourable pockets. They did well on it, the biggest being five feet long and weighing, she guessed, sixty pounds.

Since they possessed razor-like canine teeth that were like small tusks, pointing downwards, Lil was careful to avoid disturbing the critters. If they felt threatened, they would fight back *en masse*.

They were most active at dawn and dusk. During the hottest part of the day, they sought shade under the bushes, so they wouldn't overheat. She knew they couldn't survive long without water, so it was good to have the confirmation that supplies of it were at hand.

As night fell, Lil's primary concern was not for her own welfare, but for Suey-Ling and whatever it was Frenzeny and his friends might have in mind for her. The only grain of reassurance in the situation was that Suey-Ling was practised at coping with the requirements of lustful men. But this wouldn't be like a parlour house, where the most vile demands would be curbed by the supervision of a madam able to call on protection provided by a vice lord.

As the shadows deepened, Lil sneaked back to the vicinity of the Indian agency's sub-office. She clambered up the cliff-like side of a truncated sandstone spire overlooking the cabin, where she lay flat . . . and observed.

The sub-office was a good place for passing fugitives to hide out. The steep slopes behind provided a honeycomb of caves where the agency could store essentials — allegedly for the emergency sustenance of reservation Indians — house a wagon, and stable horses. The latter was especially helpful in winter when the animals' corral was snowed under, or at times when the cayuses were ones it wasn't deemed advisable to be noticed from stage-coaches.

Lil happened to know, from peering through dusty windowpanes on a previous occasion, that a door hidden behind a cupboard in the office led into a tunnel. She suspected it gave private access to the caves.

Full darkness came and lamps were lit inside the cabin. The sounds of voices and men's raucous laughter came to her on the night breeze.

Lil pondered her next move. All she could picture was a daring storming of the cabin in which she'd fling open its door and point Frenzeny's gun at them. 'You sit mighty still!' she'd cry. 'I've come for Suey-Ling.'

But that way folks were apt to end up dead. She and Suey-Ling might be among them.

She'd have to study on the breath-taking tactic and its likely outcomes a piece more before she reached a decision.

⋆ ⋆ ⋆

Jackson Farraday came back to Silver Vein on the lathered black. He took the wearied mount to the livery. The game beast quivered with fatigue.

'A fine cayuse, but he needs to rest up a whiles,' he told the hostler, indicating the gelding's glistening flanks. 'Nothing that won't be fixed with a rub-down, water . . . some oats mebbe. I'll take back the sorrel. I'm riding out again and I need a fresh bronc under me.'

He lifted off his saddle and Sam Whittaker's bag he'd confiscated from Kitty Malone. Along the trail, he'd managed to force open the padlock and had seen the bag was packed with wads of high-denomination paper money in paper bands. He transferred saddle and bag to the sorrel and mounted up.

'Kinda late fer ridin', Mr Farraday,' the hostler said, shaking his head.

'Call it early — for tomorrow,' Jackson said.

Coming down the runway and out through the barn's big double doors, he was brought to a stop by Sheriff Hamish Howard, toting a rifle. It was no mean piece of weaponry. Forty-seven inches in total, it was a Spencer lever-action repeater made to hold seven .50-calibre rimfire cartridges in a tube magazine in the buttstock.

Jackson thought, 'What kind of show is Howard putting on here?'

But it quickly transpired the lazy sheriff for once meant business. He shook the big gun, and said, 'Pull up, Jackson Farraday! The game's over. I got reason to unnerstand there's money that ain't your'n in that bag, an' a reward's been posted for your arrest!'

'What in damnation's name are you flapping your jaw about, Sheriff?' Jackson said. 'Get out of the way!'

'I'm arrestin' yuh fer armed robbery an' murder . . . hoist your hands!' Howard bellowed. 'I've had wires from

Wyoming and Green River.'

Something hellish had happened. If it was by design, he could only guess by whose.

'Don't believe 'em,' Jackson snapped, appalled. 'It's a ruse. You know I'm an honest man.'

'Yuh've turned rogue!'

'What damned foolishness! Stand aside!'

Jackson kicked and kneed the sorrel into action, forcing Howard to leap aside and surging past him.

The sheriff whirled and brought the big Spencer to his shoulder. 'Give yuhself up!' he roared.

'Go to hell!' Jackson said. He hadn't time to convince the dumb sheriff he was going off half-cocked on the basis of mistaken or fabricated information. It was imperative he got to Javelina Bend . . .

'Never thought you could be trusted for brains much further than I could spit,' he muttered angrily. 'Ain't a cent's worth of sense in your doltish, money-grasping head.'

Rocketing away, he swung his horse round a corner on to the main street.

Howard fired at him. The hasty shot ricocheted with a scream off Jackson's saddlehorn, exposing bright metal and flinging bits of leather into his face.

★ ★ ★

The sheriff let loose a stream of lurid profanity. Faces were appearing at windows and doors. A bunch of cowboys and miners, taking care to stay just within the cover of the walls of McHendry's saloon, pushed and shoved for vantage points, looking over the batwings.

Howard hollered importantly for deputies, a posse.

'Jackson Farraday's gone crazy! He's a mad-dog killer!'

A disturbed drinker spat plug-cut blackly into the street. 'Farraday the scout? Ain't you mistook some, Sheriff?'

'I ain't mistook none!' Howard declared. 'Yuh think I'm stupid? I've gotten the news by telegraph. He turned bad an' stole twenty thousan' dollars!'

The liquored-up cluster of men was impressed. Someone whistled at the back of the quickly gathering crowd.

'That's a considerable heap o' cash!'

'Where's he got it?' another asked tersely.

'He's ridin' out with it,' Howard yelled back. 'Thar's a reward. Fork leather! We'll head 'im off!'

The urgency of Howard's uncharacteristic excitement and the notion of easy money caught imaginations. Few gave thought to the argument it would make good sense to hear Jackson Farraday's side of the story.

But a calmer citizen asked, 'Sorta sudden, ain't it?'

Howard snorted. 'Never did like Farraday's holier-than-thou attitude. 'Sides, he's run, ain't he, totin' the loot? Ain't that the behaviour of a guilty man?

Drinkers and others unhitched their

ponies and flung themselves into saddles. The shrewdest knew the chase would have to be taken up fast or it would amount to nothing.

Accusation backed by the authority of a tin star became accepted truth.

Soon, a raggle-taggle string of riders was streaming out of town in Jackson's tracks, going hell-for-leather. The fool-hardy, or the drunk, smashed through brush bordering the trail, cutting corners and gaining ground.

Some maybe had hopes of collecting the reward mentioned by the sheriff; others, more unscrupulous, figured they might catch the fugitive first, grab his rich bag of loot and quit the scene in the poor light and confusion.

Glimpsing the buckskinned scout's flowing hair in the moonlight ahead of them, the detouring hotheads began firing guns.

'Fan out! Outflank him! We'll get the traitor now for sure!'

The night was split by wicked flashes and cracks.

Misfit Lil decided the odds were too heavily against the crazy notion she could walk through the door into Frenzeny's cabin and rescue Suey-Ling with one gun and the four bullets left in the chamber. She might make the first shot count, but she'd bet silver cartwheels to buttons the outlaws would fire a shot or three in return quickly enough to do her and Suey-Ling grave damage.

A showdown was in the offing, but she had sufficient sense to know more was called for than unquenchable courage.

Bold, frontal assault ruled out, Lil's thoughts returned to the caves and the tunnel from them she suspected terminated within the cabin.

The snag here was she'd never had the chance to explore the caves thoroughly — they were assumed reservation property — and it would be black as a witch's hat inside them, especially at night when any light leaking in through the faults, shafts and fissures in the broken rock would be at a minimum.

She decided she'd need a torch to have a hope of penetrating much further than a main entrance and finding a tunnel.

She scoured the brush and built the torch, using the debris of a pitchy piñon sapling recently struck by lightning and partly consumed by fire, indicating its combustible properties. Next, in the shelter of a boulder close to the caves, she gathered a small heap of tinder — crumbled wood dust from a deadfall and a quantity of small, dry twigs.

But although all this was important, it was only the first part of the job. Her pockets had been emptied, possibly by Flash Sam Whittaker or Claude Frenzeny while she'd been unconscious, and she had no matches. All she'd been left with was a half-smoked, brown-paper cigarette . . . And the four bullets in Frenzeny's gun.

She'd have to sacrifice one.

She shucked a cartridge from the revolver. The cartridge contained its own primer, and the powder was contained in a copper case with the bullet seated at the end. She removed the bullet from the cartridge and poured half the powder on her tinder. Then she put the half-empty cartridge back in the gun, without a bullet, and fired it at the tinder.

She nursed the flames and transferred them swiftly to the torch before stamping out the small fire.

Equipped with light, she flitted over the rocks and into the biggest cave. Horses in rude stalls nickered sleepily in response to the intrusion and her nostrils filled with the pungent, ammoniac stink of an unwashed and badly kept stable.

Lil took stock of, but ignored the horses. They could serve a purpose later, but hadn't their owners heard of mucking out? She moved on, entering a general storage area. She lifted the torch high and cast its pool of light this way and that.

What she discovered, revealed by the smoky, flickering flames, made her catch her breath and brought a change to her plans.

She spent a minute or two figuring out the new stunt and refining the details.

Yeah, she decided, it read real good at both first and second looks, and she was damned sure it would bring results of a spectacular kind. She chuckled and got to work.

'Frenzeny and his friends aren't going to enjoy this. They'll think the wrath of God's struck 'em!'

13

LIGHTING THE FUSES

Jackson Farraday rode from Silver Vein like the wind. Three lives might depend on a swift turn of speed; his own now added to the missing girls'.

Twice, the pursuers were close at his heels. A reckless party had swung out early and cut across brush before angling in again. The attempt to overhaul and head him off nearly succeeded.

A burst of gunfire sent lead whistling around him in a potentially lethal gale. He ducked and dodged in the saddle as best he could, but a bullet ripped his clothing, scraped his ribs and left a sore gash, bleeding but not badly. No bone was broken, he thought. He swivelled round and shot back.

The results of such an exchange on

horseback were always in the lap of the gods, but Jackson had the satisfaction of seeing one leading horse break its pace and swerve, whinnying shrilly. The rider's attempt to haul up and control it made it rear. A pile-up resulted that unseated three riders and sent three horses rolling. The air was made blue with wrathful curses.

Jackson hurtled on. When he'd left the party a hundred yards in the rear, it made a last bid to ventilate him.

A toppled posseman hauled himself up from the dust. He yelled, 'Smoke him down, boys!'

A scattered firing chopped into the brush and raised puffs of dust on the trail behind Jackson, but the bunch was deterred and he was out of immediate danger.

Though familiar in his Army work with riding in darkness or mist over rough country, Jackson held to the stage road, reckoning it to be the fastest route into the canyonlands and to the cabin at Javelina Bend.

At first, he passed the properties of legitimate ranchers and settlers, but further from town few were hanging on in the face of outlawry and well-armed, renegade Indians. Isolated homes had been deserted and were tumbling down.

It was a bleak reminder to Jackson of the ruin visited upon the country by LOOO, Flash Sam Whittaker and Claude Frenzeny. The last had yet to be brought to book for his misdeeds and was effectively being abetted by the incompetent Sheriff Howard, who'd collected payoffs from Flash Sam and Kitty Malone for nodding at their infringements of ordinances.

Jackson didn't think Howard was aware of the Silver Vein pair's more heinous crimes centred around the gunrunning, Jimmie Sanders and the Indian agent. He was a tinhorn and he'd been duped by Kitty one last time.

What a stupid, dull-witted fool the man had been to be taken in by her telegrams!

The hill country became less wooded and more broken, gashed by ravines and gullies, accented by jagged-topped, eroded ridges. Barren crags overhung the trail, looming a denser black against the starry sky.

A bare mile from Javelina Bend, when the sky was taking on the pallid hue of false dawn, the frontrunners of Howard's makeshift posse, the ones who possessed or had commandeered the saltiest horses, drew within firing range a second time. The cracks of gunfire echoed through the rocky landscape.

Jackson realized he'd be able to do two captive girls no good whatever if he arrived at the cabin only to be cut down or arrested by Howard and his hangers-on.

Turning a bend that momentarily shielded him from his hunters, he saw a trailside niche in the rocks, filled with scrub growth. Desperately, he yanked at the reins and guided the sorrel into it. Making little sound, he backed the

191

horse further into the bushes and dismounted. He held his hand over the horse's muzzle in the known command that it should make no betraying whinny of salute to the posse's broncs.

He hunkered down in the shadows of the rocks, holding his breath in the hope Howard's men would plunge on downtrail and pass the Javelina Bend outpost without stopping.

But he was out of luck. A sharp-eyed rannie spotted the broken bushes. Jackson groaned as he exultantly announced his discovery.

'Hey! Lookee here, pards!' the man cried. 'Reck'n he's gone inta hidin'!'

The group milled and several members brought their horses to a standstill and swung from their saddles, guns in hand.

Jackson retreated further into the undergrowth, alarmed at the crackling as his boots crunched down on the dried twigs underfoot.

Three shots crashed out almost as one as the possemen fired at the sound, cutting the shadows with red flame. Jackson felt the heat of the lead as it zipped by him. He answered with deterring fire of his own.

Then, startlingly, the earth trembled and the air shook with the rolling thunder of a series of reverberating explosions.

★   ★   ★

When Misfit Lil saw the two wooden crates at the back of the cave she was transfixed, but only for seconds before she set to work with a new will.

Each crate was stencilled in black, 'Dynamite'. The stuff was surely a godsend!

'It'll be just the thing to settle them varmints' hash,' she said to herself. 'Just hang on, Suey-Ling — I'll be coming to save you.'

Lil was no expert with explosives. She knew you were liable to blow yourself up if you monkeyed around with dynamite. But she remembered happy days at the Flying G when she'd watched her father's hands at work clearing trees from land reclaimed from woodland for pasture.

Two eager men had determined to get rid of a troublesome stump fast — using dynamite. They'd known the principles of handling it, but were hazy on how much was called for. They dug down to the tap root and placed six sticks of sixty per cent dynamite. The stump was blown to glory. Lil could still see the thousand particles dispersing far and wide. The hands worked the rest of the day filling the hole.

The dynamite here was probably what was left of a batch used for a similar land-clearing purpose on the reservation. A few, unexpected explosions of the type she'd witnessed on the Flying G would be plenty to rattle Frenzeny and his friends. If they were close enough to the cabin, they'd be alarmed sufficiently to rush out for safety, or at least to learn what the hell was going on. From there on, she'd have to play her cards as they fell.

She broke open the crates by the unsteady light of her torch and laid out eighteen yellow-wrapped sticks of dynamite in batches of six with blasting caps. To two of the bundles she made she attached long lengths of fuse — enough to give her a count to twenty, as she'd seen it done on the Flying G. The third she gave a much shorter fuse. She crimped all the caps and fuses tight to the bundles and split the ends for easier lighting.

Lil then took out the half-smoked quirly overlooked in her emptied pockets and lit it from the torch, drawing and puffing till its glow was steady and reliable.

The Javelina Bend sub-office, though a single, isolated building, in fact had two minor structures attached. The largest was a privy to the south, fashioned from sheets of corrugated roofing iron; the other was a wellhouse on the side away from the road. Both sat close to the house.

The sky was already lightening and Lil would have to work fast to utilize the remaining cover of darkness. She extinguished the pine torch and left the caves.

Lil scooted through the rocks, using all available cover she could, till it was necessary to streak across the open, last hundred yards to the privy.

A lamp was still lit inside the cabin. The men had made a night of it, it seemed. She heard scuffling and low guffaws of amusement. A woman's muffled moan that had to be made by Suey-Ling was followed by male cries of lewd self-congratulation and back-slapping.

The swine! Well, they were going to get a shock and the unfortunate Oriental girl with whom they were having their way would be spared further harm. If this stunt came off aright, the trio wouldn't have the stomach for toying with women or much else.

Her approach hadn't been detected

by the busy molesters. She eased open the privy door and pushed in a bundle of dynamite, then backed off, unravelling its long fuse. When she reached the end of it, she took the cigarette from her pursed lips and touched the red end to the fuse.

The fuse lit brightly, died, then spluttered into a more regular life. A line of sparks started on their way along the fuse, fizzing and giving off a small stream of white smoke.

The game was afoot. Already breathless with excitement and anxiety, Lil darted round the cabin to the wellhouse and shoved the second bundle of dynamite up between the roof and a supporting rafter. She lit its fuse; ran again.

She ignited the short fuse to the last bundle with the shrinking, glowing remains of the cigarette and flung it hissing under the cabin's porch steps. Ran . . .

From somewhere in the near distance, she thought she heard a crackle of gunfire. But immediately she was effectively deafened to everything but her own handiwork.

Split seconds after she'd gained the shelter of boulders across the road from the cabin, the privy blew up with an almighty roar and flash. Pieces of sheet iron flew in every direction. Some of the debris smashed on to the cabin; some fragments sailed over her own head.

She had the fuses timed well. Little more than a heartbeat later, the wellhouse and the porch steps also disintegrated with two more closely spaced booms that made Lil's ears ring. Shattered wellhead bricks and splintered timber were tossed high, rained down.

The cabin was obscured by a swirling cloud of dust and smoke, but Lil watched closely in tense anticipation.

Fearing for their lives, the outlaw pair bolted out over the flattened door of the cabin in a state of partial undress, one pulling suspenders on to his shoulders.

Both carried pistols and clearly supposed they were under some form of attack on all sides, possibly from the law that hunted them.

'What the hell's happened?' one asked, peering through the dark murk.

With a hollow, singing sound still in his head, his scowling but nervous companion was in no mind to guess.

'Who knows? Don't make no sense to stay fer a siege! Let's get outa here!'

Frenzeny appeared in the busted doorway, boiling with rage. Apparently only he had a glimmering of what had been done and by whom.

'It must be the other gal!' he yelled at the top of his lungs after the fleeing pair. 'She's behind this vandalism. Misfit Lil's gotta be out there someplace. It's only one gal, I tell you!'

But Frenzeny's visitors were figuring it for themselves. With furtive, hunted glances all around at the impressive spread of wreckage, they discounted the shouted explanation.

One unassisted girl could achieve

such devastation? Yeah, like coyotes could fly!

They knew Frenzeny for a smooth-talking twister, but he couldn't expect anyone but a damned fool to believe what he was trying to sell them this time.

This was like war. In horror, they smelled the reek of explosives, and feared the next blast would dispatch them to another place. Any kingdom-come for which they'd be worthy would be an even fierier, more sulphurous place.

They sprinted for the caves and their horses.

Misfit Lil saw it was time to use one of the three shots she had left in Frenzeny's revolver. She took aim at the leading outlaw and triggered. The gun roared.

The bullet took the outlaw high in the right leg and flung him off his feet. He crashed down heavily in a dust-raising heap.

'Aagh! Goddamn, I been hit, Sly!

Don't leave me!'

Lil drew a bead on the hesitating Sly, preparing to place another telling shot. But she never got to squeeze the trigger.

What happened next was totally unexpected. It was outside even Lil's reckoning, and created fresh panic all round.

14

STAND AT JAVELINA BEND

Angry-he-shakes-fist was no ordinary mortal. Friend and foe were struck by the man's force of character. A young delinquent from an Apache sub-tribe, he'd jumped the reservation in search of better living, excitement and the satisfaction of self-pride. His undeniable charisma had drawn to him a band of mostly young bucks eager for adventure and the lost freedom of their kind's older ways.

Angry-fist had raided the white man's horse and cattle herds, torched isolated settlements, attacked trains of freight wagons. He'd garnered food, horses and a lot of ammunition, and the wrath of the Army. He'd led blue-clad cavalry troopers many a dance through inhospitable country that drained their energy and sapped their spirits.

But his cause was ultimately vested with a desperate futility and when he'd come up against white-eye opponents with the courage and skills of Jackson Farraday and Misfit Lil, he met his match. He also lost a hand to the white frontiersman in a duel fought with tomahawks.

Ironically, he was left with but one fist to shake; chillingly, a deeper bitterness characterized his subsequent campaigns. Anger became unremitting rage. Ferocity seethed in his savage heart. Eluding the military, he vowed to be avenged on scout Farraday.

His cunning sharpened by his misfortunes, Angry-fist dickered with corrupt white men. In exchange for direction over attacks on their own kind, they supplied him and his marauders with trinkets and — more importantly — firearms of the latest design. He couldn't grow a new hand, but he could grow his power and standing. He was still chief among his braves; with the new guns, he could be the mightiest warrior under the sun.

Day and night, he and his men kept tireless watch on the often baffling activities of the white men remaining in the ever-lonelier country around the hated reservation, Fort Dennis and Silver Vein. It was thus by no stroke of luck that the redskin renegades observed both the explosions at Javelina Bend and the running gunfight waged between a ragtag group of white riders and — oh, praise to Usen! — the white arch-enemy, Jackson Farraday. His flowing yellow hair and sorrel horse were recognizable at considerable distance.

As the moon sank in the star-studded heavens, both remarkable incidents came under eagle-like scrutiny. High on a commanding ridge, Angry-fist saw a chance for possible useful plunder. The Indian agent and his friends did not speak with straight tongues. Plainly they had a store of the powerful sticks of fire powder at Javelina Bend. This, they had previously denied to him.

Moreover, as the white men's chase converged on the agency sub-office, Angry-fist anticipated vengeance at last against Jackson Farraday. It was time for he and his men to ride down on their swift-footed mustangs and play a part in the developing conflict.

'They make much noise, carried to us because the wind is right,' he remarked. 'They will not hear our approach. Nor will they see us. The fools' eyes are turned away and their sight is too weak for them to see us until it is too late.'

A party two-dozen strong sent their half-broken ponies slithering pell-mell down the scree-covered slopes from their elevated lookout post and a nearby encampment.

★ ★ ★

When the pre-dawn air was rent by three deafeningly huge explosions close by, the trigger-happy posse led by

Sheriff Hamish Howard was momentarily thrown into confusion.

They whirled about and spotted a black cloud rising further down the stage road.

'What in thunder's name is that?'

'*Thunder* it ain't, Sheriff. It's explosives.'

The respite in the one-sided gunfight enabled Jackson Farraday to swing astride the sorrel. His aim was to take maximum advantage of his surprise chance to ride out fast, though he, too, was bewildered by the blasts. They'd occurred down the road a piece, at Javelina Bend for sure. He was alarmed at what they might signify. His thoughts went instantly to the kidnapped girls.

He crashed his bronc through more brush in the direction of the Indian agency's sub-office, disregarding whether it was the best course for saving his own damaged skin. He felt scorching heat from the bullet graze on his side. When he put fingers to his ribs the blood was warm and sticky to his touch but not pumping out the furrow. He knew intuitively it wasn't a serious injury just as he knew in his unbroken bones events were moving toward a climax.

Not fifty yards ridden and rejoining the road via another cutoff, he heard the blundering possemen pounding after him.

He was giving rapid, anxious thought as to whether he was rushing into trouble or out of it when a new peril surged into view.

Trouble was a-building all right! A raiding party of renegade Indians led by the ruthless Angry-fist himself came streaming toward the road across a slope directly to the right.

When they realized they'd been spotted by both Jackson and his pursuers at the same time, the rebel warriors broke into an unruly charge, whooping and shrieking.

A couple of shots from the hostiles' repeating rifles missed Jackson by inches, but one of Howard's men was knocked out of his saddle by the same volley of gunfire. His left foot stayed caught up in the stirrup. His horse went frantic. Uncontrolled, it galloped wildly toward the Indians, dragging its rider's corpse.

The band swerved and parted to avoid collision, but one of the wiry ponies tripped and went down. The redskin owner was pitched off and screamed as the pony rolled on him. The animal promptly scrambled to its feet, forcing other speeding redskins to take evasive action. They snarled in rage at the disarray forced upon them by the loose horses.

The shock of the Indian attack brought an abrupt end to the pursuit of Jackson. Self-preservation was the first and only object in anyone's mind.

Sheriff Howard had enough sense to figure survival could depend on mounting a mutual defence against the rebel redmen. He also deduced, wrongly in part, that the intended target of their raid must have been the reservation's sub-office before Farraday had inadvertently led the posse on to the scene.

'Shoot only at the 'Paches!' he bellowed. 'We'll make a stand at the agency post!'

But the Indians, though a number were presently confounded, were already regrouping.

* * *

Misfit Lil's hand was stayed when the crackle of gunfire she'd heard swelled into a vigorous, approaching exchange and was augmented by eerily blood-curdling war-cries.

An Indian attack!

To expend her last two shots at such a moment would be crazy. Lil was no faintheart, but many a strong-minded frontierswoman advised a white lady's last bullet should be kept to take her own life lest worsening circumstances demanded it as the only escape from rape, torture and death.

Frenzeny, Sly and his sidekick also heard the Indians' cries and the racket of guns. Frenzeny went into a panic.

'Angry-fist must've gone out of his mind!' he rapped. 'Back to the cabin!'

The man Lil had crippled screamed, 'No — don't leave me! My leg's smashed, yuh dumbheads! Drag me inta the rocks.'

'Shuddup, Leet!' Sly said. 'There's guns and ammo in the cabin. We'll need everythin' we got to hold 'em off!'

He scurried back to the partly wrecked but still solid cabin in the wake of the paunchy Indian agent.

'Looks like your fine pards are leaving you to me or the Injuns, Leet,' Lil called. 'Promise not to shoot and I'll give you my shoulder to lean on.'

Leet groaned and gave his hasty agreement. 'Sure, kid! I got no beef with yuh — God's truth!'

'You'll have to hop real quick!' Lil told him. She thrust the revolver back in her waistband and hauled him on to his good leg.

The cabin with its door blown in by dynamite was a dubious place of refuge and defence, but Lil preferred it and

210

any loaded guns it stocked to the rocks and the two bullets in her snatched revolver.

An acute worry was that Frenzeny would cut her down anyhow, Indian attack or not, but she kept close to Leet, supporting his body in a way it might deter this treachery by the Indian agent to a woman of his own race.

Her dread she'd be shot by Frenzeny was short-lived. Suddenly, Jackson Farraday arrived on his sorrel at a furious gallop. He reined in to a rearing halt. She'd never been more surprised or pleased to see him. He leaped down and slapped his horse on the rump, sending it charging away riderless.

'That's right, Miss Lilian! Angry-fist's on the war-trail — everyone to the cabin!'

Farraday was followed hotfoot by Sheriff Hamish Howard and a motley group of armed men. With the unexpected but welcome help, Lil made it to the cabin. Leet — a tall, gangling fellow — rested his right arm across her shoulder for support.

They piled in and the broken door was manhandled roughly into place and barricaded with a heavy desk.

Howard checked off his posse. 'Where're the rest?' he asked.

'One got shot out of the saddle,' Jackson said. 'He was dragged and must be dead.'

'Five couldn't keep up an' turned back earlier,' a posseman volunteered.

'That leaves only one unaccounted by my reckonin',' Howard said.

Lil thought it was typical of Howard not to have his priorities in order. 'Ain't no time for doing sums, Sheriff. I ain't properly heeled. Get Frenzeny to break out some weaponry.'

Frenzeny's face tightened. A fire of pure hatred burned in his eyes. 'We letting gals tell us what to do?'

'Yeah,' Jackson interposed. 'Move it, Frenzeny! Don't you know we need every gun? Give Lil a rifle. She's the best shooter in the territory.'

Lil said, 'The gun rack's in the end

part of the cabin, behind them strung blankets.'

The blankets partitioned the cabin, maybe cordoning off a sleeping area. In present circumstances, they served no good use. Outside, Angry-fist's gleeful warriors were circling the cabin, yelling like fiends from the Pit. Challenging shots thudded into the stout walls of the cabin. More spanged off the gabled iron roof.

Frenzeny, scowling darkly, ineffectively tried to bar the way of two possemen. 'Keep back from there — it's private!'

'We need all the guns and ammo in the place, mister!'

The men pushed past him, grabbed the blankets and tore them down.

The pair were shaken by what they saw. They stared, open-mouthed.

'*Jesus!* What goes on here?'

'Awful! Jest awful . . . '

Shock and disgust swept through the cabin. The fall of the blankets had revealed a ghastly tableau hidden

213

behind them. It was sufficient to distract from the devilish horror of attacking Apaches. It brought the bile of anger to rough men's throats; the moistness of pity to their eyes.

The young Oriental prostitute Suey-Ling, a familiar, distinctive figure in Silver Vein, was barely conscious, faint heartbeats from death. Her face was discoloured, badly bruised where someone had hit her. She'd been hung by her tied wrists from a rafter, arms outstretched. Each delicate ankle had been separately tied and the free ends of the thick ropes secured by heavy nails, hammered into the floor a yard apart.

Blood dripped on to the tatters of her clothing, dumped in a heap between her feet.

Lil felt numb. The way the naked girl had been secured in the shape of an X had opened her completely to Frenzeny's, Sly's and Leet's cruel attentions.

'It — it was Frenzeny,' Leet stammered. 'It was all his idea. I swear I wanted to be gentle with her.'

'Kill the bastards!' someone cried.

His face tight with controlled wrath, Jackson said commandingly, 'In due time — if Angry-fist leaves us the chance. The damned perverts can't get away. Some of you get her down. The rest, take up positions at the windows.'

Lil and two of the men cut the ropes and lowered Suey-Ling to the floor. Lil saw her wrists were rubbed raw from her struggles; they'd bled on to the ropes. She cradled the girl's head and put a whiskey flask she'd been handed to her bruised and torn lips.

The rest of the besieged party took up rifles, steadying them against window frame and door jamb. They fired rapidly, working levers as fast as they could, yet making their shots tell.

Lil itched to join the fray, but had to content herself with glimpses of the action through a broken window.

Angry-fist followed his usual tactic of whipping his young, impressionable followers into a frenzy. Oblivious to the defenders' return fire, a charging savage would rush in recklessly, often to be dropped from his horse by a hail of bullets.

Lil made Suey-Ling as comfortable as she could and reloaded Frenzeny's revolver from what was left of the stock of shells that had been stored with the cabin's scanty armaments. She also appropriated a triggerless Colt Frontier ignored by the others.

Frontiers left the factory in Connecticut complete with triggers, but some gunslicks of the stripe who rode the Outlaw Trail, holing up with Frenzeny's help along the way, were inclined to dispense with them. Their debatable contention was triggers were slow in operation and it was better to thumb the hammer, giving themselves a split-second's edge.

Equipped with the two guns, Lil felt more ready to do battle. She settled herself alongside others below a window.

The red rebels had given up hope of rushing the cabin in the face of the defenders' concerted fire. She saw they were playing for time. Angry-fist had them circling endlessly on their ponies, taunting and jeering, hoping to lure the white men into using up ammunition to no effect on fleeting targets.

Lil suspected the raiding party's supply of cartridges could be dwindling, too, and that for both sides the outcome was in question. She calculated about half the Indians had modern repeaters which gave them sixteen shots in a full magazine.

How many had they already wasted in their undisciplined enthusiasm? How long could the white men hold out?

While she was debating the imponderables with herself, she caught furtive movement within the room from the corner of her eye. All attention was on the Indians outside . . . except Claude Frenzeny's.

The crooked Indian agent had eased back the cupboard that hid the tunnel to the caves and was squeezing through the gap.

15

HOGGING THE ACTION

'Hey!' Lil burst forth. 'Stop Frenzeny, somebody! The stinking rat is making off!'

She turned Frenzeny's revolver but didn't dare fire across the crowded room. A cowhand flung himself after the escaping rogue. He was too late. Frenzeny was already through the gap, dragging the cupboard back almost to its former position.

He and another posseman began shifting it, then backed off hurriedly when a single shot was fired from inside the mouth of the tunnel. The heavy bullet punched a splintery hole through the cupboard's wooden panels and creased the cowhand's right arm. He looked at the blood and cursed ripely.

'I've got an answer for that,' Lil

gritted. She went over and fired three rapid shots through the cupboard with Frenzeny's revolver.

'Where's he gone?' Jackson asked.

'Through to some caves in the hillside. He's got horses stashed there,' Lil said. 'Get the cupboard moved — I'm going after the two-legged skunk.'

'You sure that ain't suicide?'

'I'm going in firing and it might be for him,' Lil promised grimly.

'Wish yuh luck, Misfit Lil,' the wounded cowhand said. He was tying a bandanna round the top of his bleeding arm. 'Make the misbegotten bastard pay!'

When the cupboard was cautiously pulled clear, Lil split the darkness inside with the flashes of her two guns. The din deafened and reverberated. But when it subsided, of Frenzeny there was no evidence, dead or alive. After firing his warning shot, he'd lost no time in scrambling through the claustrophobic escape route to the caves.

Lil groped and stumbled up the dark passage herself, heading for a patch of grey ahead. She barked her shins against jagged rocks and bounced off walls that grazed her outstretched hands.

Doggedly, she pressed on, knowing the tunnel didn't run far.

Hope the Indians see Frenzeny and perforate his rotten yellow hide, she thought. She doubted it though. If he rode in the cabin's direction, he knew he'd be caught in a crossfire with white men's guns likewise turned on him. Western men of character — even rough character — were hard on men who abused women, even prostitutes.

He'd inflicted unspeakable torture on Suey-Ling. He'd be punished mercilessly.

If some of the worthies who'd tried to educate her in Boston were believed, a body was liable to burn in hell for considerably less than what Frenzeny had done.

She came to the smelly cave where

the horses were stabled. The two draught animals for the wagon were there, but one of the two outlaws' saddle mounts was gone.

She took the time to throw a saddle across the pair's bronc that had been left and rode out, eyes peeled for fresh hoofprints. She expected Frenzeny to shun the made roads altogether and ride across country.

He would no longer have a life to live in this country. He'd want to ride fast and far to quit the consequences of his despicable actions. But first he'd have to dodge Angry-fist and his warriors, unless he could count somehow on their recognizing a lone, fleeing white rider as an erstwhile friend. That limited the routes he could take through the maze of canyons without losing himself.

It was still semi-dark, but a greyness in the east told of approaching day. In the pale dawn light, sharp-eyed Lil picked up tracks in the chaos of rocks and brush. She drew in her breath sharply.

'Oh, no, you dirty traitor, this way you ain't going cautious at all. Seeing how the critters you should be minding have a very good nose . . . '

She worked forward herself with more patience and stealth than an Indian. She brought into play every trick of woodcraft she knew to make her own progress discreet.

Moving into a deep gully, filled with concealing brush, she paused. She tutted. 'A greenhorn like you ain't got any business straying into a place like this.'

She spied freshly broken twigs at horsehead height. In a patch of softer sand and clay filling a hollow in the rocky ground of a small clearing, she saw the imprint of hoofs. Sure now she was on the right trail, she paused again to listen. A travelling man is almost certain to make sound detectable within a reasonable distance, and she reckoned she must be getting close to her quarry.

She was rewarded with the sounds of

crackling brush and a horse's snorts of disapproval of the path it was being forced to take.

'Fool, you're just asking for trouble,' she breathed.

She pulled the two borrowed guns from her waist-band — the one with a trigger, the other without. Her thoughts raced.

The ill-chosen route was likely to land both Frenzeny and herself in a fine how-d'you-do. Did Frenzeny know how dangerous it was to plunge willy-nilly through this particular thicket? Should she warn him? Fire warning shots? Cry out?

Abruptly, the moment to make any decision of that ilk was past.

The disaster began with a snarling and snorting that sounded like a cacophony of rude blasts on bugles played by a lineup of raw Army recruits.

She heard Frenzeny berating his horse, which whinnied shrilly in fear.

'Where'd Leet get you, you baulky cayuse? Keep going! Ain't nothing but pigs — a mess of damn pork!'

The words were ominous to Lil. The arrogant fool! If Frenzeny thought his horse was scaring too easily, he was very wrong. And before long, if he persisted, he was likely to be dead wrong.

The pigs were peccaries or musk hogs — the javelinas who inhabited this part of the country and gave the Indian agency's sub-office at the bend in the stage road its name.

Javelinas were the wild pigs of North America. They looked like domestic pigs; barrel-shaped and covered with short, blackish-grey bristly hair. But in fact they were none too closely related. They were bigger beasts, weighing up to sixty pounds and growing to five feet in length from rubbery snout to smelly rump. They had small, round ears and vicious, beady eyes. And razor-like, pointed canine teeth. Tusks . . .

Lil understood the word javelina had its roots in a Spanish word for spear.

She avoided disturbing javelinas,

since she'd found them to be exception-ally mean beasts. They always lived in packs of fifteen to twenty, and when they came under apparent attack, they fought back with a formidable will.

The skunk-like smell with which the javelinas marked out their territory should alone have warned Frenzeny away. But now he'd bought into some real trouble.

'Goddamnit! Hold hard, you skittish jughead! Here, I'll deal to these varmints!'

A gun was fired giving rise to a chorus of angry woofing sounds in response.

Lil heard an equine squeal of pain and terror, and the crash of a body falling into undergrowth.

'Cuss it!' Frenzeny blazed.

Moments later, Frenzeny's spooked horse bolted riderless through the clearing where Lil stood transfixed. It had bloody fetlocks that looked like they might have been ripped. Or chewed on.

She pulled her own horse aside on a tight rein and backed into a stand of more substantial scrub oaks.

Second and third shots were fired, then Frenzeny himself came smashing through the undergrowth. He was scarcely looking where he was going. His head was turned fearfully and his smoking gun was raised on an extended arm, pointing behind him.

Shooting won't stop them, Lil thought. She'd seen javelinas keep right on running when their bodies were filled with lead. They were tenacious, stubborn brutes. The only thing they wouldn't do once their dander was up was run *away*. When a javelina died, it sure died game.

Lil had a theory their natural breeding was suspect. The young born to the females of a group travelled with it their whole life until they died. No new members were ever accepted into the group unless they are born into it. Was their vicious disposition the result of inbreeding?

Right enough, the disaster unfolded with a bunch of the hogs bursting into the clearing on Frenzeny's heels. They had short, hooved legs, but they moved faster than most running men.

They'd been disturbed, trespassed upon. Their females had likely been nursing their waking twin young. They were on the attack.

Frenzeny screamed at them. 'Leave me alone! Get back, filth!'

Inevitably in his panic, Frenzeny tripped.

He fell, shrieking, but leaped quickly to his feet, only to be bowled over by the lead hog, a massive beast, more than two feet high at the shoulder. The javelina gored his leg and when he lurched up again, he was limping, off-balance. Two, three paces and a tide of the stocky, grey-black bodies bore him down. This time he couldn't get up. He was trampled and smashed under the hoofs. The wicked tusks stabbed into his flesh.

He expended the last two shots in his

six-gun. The gully sent roaring echoes of his fire crashing from wall to wall. Before they faded, he was screaming in a chilling, high falsetto.

Lil at first shut her eyes instinctively. She was not a squeamish girl and had seen more than her fair share of spilled blood, yet she had to force herself to look.

She levelled her two guns, then she faltered, shrugged and let them fall to her sides, unfired. It was unpleasant, gruesome, but what the hell? Let the hogs get on with it. When pig met pigs, maybe it was best not to interfere. Maybe Frenzeny's was a deserved fate. Nor did she want to bring the javelinas' wrath down on her own head.

Dazed, racked with pain, Frenzeny sobbed profane curses as he tried to drag himself away from the ravening beasts. Mercifully, his reeling senses left him quickly.

Lil watched, her stomach turning. The javelinas thrust in their pointed heads and disc-like noses, snuffling and grunting eagerly. Long tusks ripped away. In a matter of minutes, Frenzeny was reduced to rags and white bone and livid gore. A grotesque, broken figure. A terrible, sickening sight.

She turned her borrowed horse and got out of there while the getting was good.

Disrespecting the wilderness was no sin of Misfit Lil's.

* * *

Lil rode back to the Javelina Bend sub-office as fast as the country would permit. But her absence had been longer than she'd realized and events there were moving swiftly to a climax.

First, she heard the sound of an Army bugler sounding the charge. She urged her horse to higher ground. Topping a ridge, she was in time to witness a detachment of cavalry coming to the relief of the besieged party at the Indian agency cabin — still managing to raise a withering defensive fire.

229

The cavalry thundered up, the rising sun revealing their blue coats and winking off the metal of uniform buttons and insignia and the horses' bridle gear. Angry-fist, sitting erect and haughty overseeing his warriors' swoops, signalled his force to break off the attack with a gesture of frustration. His braves, fearing they'd be caught in a deadly crossfire, halted in their tracks and wheeled in retreat.

Within moments, the rebel Indians were swallowed up in the canyonlands as though they'd disappeared off the face of the inhospitable land. The troopers gave chase, but Lil knew the effort to apprehend Angry-fist would prove as futile as always.

Some hours later, Jackson Farraday explained to her what had happened.

'Seems the man from his posse Sheriff Howard couldn't account for dodged the redskins and raced to Fort Dennis for help.'

Lieutenant Michael Covington, who'd led the rescue column in person, seemed

230

to preen himself as he brushed dust from his dark-blue coat and sky-blue trousers.

'The man winded his horse, but it was as well. We were just in time to save the day.'

'Don't claim all the credit, Lieutenant,' Farraday said. 'Miss Lilian Goodnight here played a hand in bringing the sorry business to an end. She saw how Jimmie Sanders was duped, maybe she spurred Flash Sam and Kitty Malone into running out on the evil conspiracy, and she was surely on Claude Frenzeny's tail at the end.'

Covington hemmed. 'She doesn't miss a trick, does she?' he said. 'Maybe you're right, but I don't know about the propriety of it.'

'Oh, you and your precious propriety, Mike!' Lil said, turning on him. 'And don't patronize me either.'

Covington flinched at the 'Mike', hating the diminutive and the disrespectful familiarity it implied.

'Pah! You'll bite off more than you

can chew one day, Miss Goodnight.'

'Huh! If'n that's so, it's because I'll be attending to something you couldn't get your pearly teeth into fast enough, Mike. Go to hell!'

A jaw muscle twitched in the handsome young man's tightened face. He pulled back on his leather gauntleted gloves and strode away stiff-legged in calf-high black boots.

Jackson sighed. 'Now why did you have to go upsetting him? He really is a fine fellow, you know. If you just tried being polite, he might react more friendly.'

Lil didn't know that it was Mike Covington she wanted to be more friendly. But she had to admit the lieutenant did look kind of dashing, from the neat, tucked-in folds of the kerchief about his neck down to the gloss of his boots. Could anyone look so good and be the truth? And did he have to be so uncompromisingly proud of his spit-and-polish reputation; always expect her to act like an Eastern lady?

'Yeah, well . . . ' she said to Jackson, 'at least this time he couldn't accuse me of hogging the action. I was outdone by musk hogs. The javelinas made a swill meal of Frenzeny.'

She shuddered and put the picture firmly out of her mind.

Unlike the continuing problem of what a girl was to do about Mike Covington and Jackson Farraday, it was over.

THE END

We do hope that you have enjoyed reading this large print book.

Did you know that all of our titles are available for purchase?

We publish a wide range of high quality large print books including:
**Romances, Mysteries, Classics
General Fiction
Non Fiction and Westerns**

Special interest titles available in large print are:
**The Little Oxford Dictionary
Music Book, Song Book
Hymn Book, Service Book**

Also available from us courtesy of Oxford University Press:
**Young Readers' Dictionary
(large print edition)
Young Readers' Thesaurus
(large print edition)**

For further information or a free brochure, please contact us at:
**Ulverscroft Large Print Books Ltd.,
The Green, Bradgate Road, Anstey,
Leicester, LE7 7FU, England.
Tel:** (00 44) **0116 236 4325
Fax:** (00 44) **0116 234 0205**